Stay where you are and then Leave

www.randomhousechildrens.co.uk

Also by John Boyne

Novels:
The Thief of Time
The Congress of Rough Riders
Crippen
Next of Kin
Mutiny on the Bounty
The House of Special Purpose
The Absolutist
This House is Haunted

Novels for Younger Readers:
The Boy in the Striped Pyjamas
Noah Barleywater Runs Away
The Terrible Thing That Happened
to Barnaby Brocket

Stay where you are and then Leave

JOHN BOYNE

With chapter titles hand-lettered by Oliver Jeffers

CORGI BOOKS

Praise for John Boyne

Stay Where You Are and Then Leave

'Wonderful . . . one of the best books of the year. An instant classic' Eoin Colfer

'A beautifully paced and touching tale' *Mail on Sunday*

'Poignantly enlightening' *Independent on Sunday*

The Terrible Thing That Happened to Barnaby Brocket

'An uplifting celebration of otherness' *Daily Mail*

'A whimsical, warm-hearted adventure . . . beautifully illustrated' *The Bookseller*

'Funny, warm, but poignant . . . a tribute to the power of the imagination' *Booktrust*

The Boy in the Striped Pyjamas

'A small wonder of a book' *Guardian*

'An extraordinary book . . . a powerful story, simply told' *Irish Examiner*

'Quite impossible to put down, this is the rare kind of book that doesn't leave your head for days' *The Bookseller*

Noah Barleywater Runs Away

'Destined to become something of a children's classic' *Mail on Sunday*

'Sparkling . . . highly amusing, refreshingly original and extremely moving . . . fizzes with energy and ideas' *Guardian*

'Spellbinding stuff' *Financial Times*

STAY WHERE YOU ARE AND THEN LEAVE
A CORGI BOOK 978 0 552 57058 9

First published in Great Britain by Doubleday,
an imprint of of Random House Children's Publishers UK
A Random House Group Company

Hardback edition published 2013
This edition published 2014

3 5 7 9 10 8 6 4

The Random House Group Limited supports The Forest Stewardship Council® (FSC®), the leading international forest-certification organisation. Our books carrying the FSC label are printed on FSC®-certified paper. FSC is the only forest-certification scheme supported by the leading environmental organisations, including Greenpeace. Our paper procurement policy can be found at www.randomhouse.co.uk/environment

Set in New Baskerville

Corgi Books are published by Random House Children's Publishers UK,
61-63 Uxbridge Road, London, W5 5SA

www.**randomhousechildrens**.co.uk
www.**totallyrandombooks**.co.uk
www.**randomhouse**.co.uk

Addresses for companies within The Random House Group Limited can be found at: www.randomhouse.co.uk/offices.htm

THE RANDOM HOUSE GROUP Limited Reg. No. 954009

A CIP catalogue record for this book is available from the British Library.

Printed and bound in Great Britain by CPI Group (UK) Ltd, Croydon, CR0 4YY

For my parents

1

SEND ME AWAY WITH A SMILE

Every night, before he went to sleep, Alfie Summerfield tried to remember how life had been before the war began. And with every passing day, it became harder and harder to keep the memories clear in his head.

The fighting had started on 28 July 1914. Others might not have remembered that date so easily but Alfie would never forget it, for that was his birthday. He had turned five years old that day and his parents threw him a party to celebrate, but only a handful of people showed up: Granny Summerfield, who sat in the corner, weeping into her handkerchief and saying, 'We're finished, we're all finished,' over and over, until Alfie's mum said that if she couldn't get a hold of herself she would have to leave; Old Bill Hemperton, the Australian from next door, who was about a hundred years old and played a trick with his false teeth, sliding them in and out of his mouth using nothing but his tongue; Alfie's best friend, Kalena Janáček, who lived three doors down at number six, and her father, who ran the sweet shop on the corner and had the shiniest shoes in London. Alfie invited most of his friends from Damley Road, but that morning, one by one, their mothers knocked on the Summerfields' front door and said that little So-and-so wouldn't be able to come.

'It's not a day for a party, is it?' asked Mrs Smythe from number nine, the mother of Henry Smythe, who sat in the seat in front of Alfie in school and made at least ten disgusting smells every day. 'It's best if you just cancel it, dear.'

'I'm not cancelling anything,' said Alfie's mother, Margie, throwing up her hands in frustration after the fifth parent had come to call. 'If anything, we should be doing our best to have a good time today. And what am I to do with all this grub if no one shows up?'

Alfie followed her into the kitchen and looked at the table, where corned-beef sandwiches, stewed tripe, pickled eggs, cold tongue and jellied eels were all laid out in a neat row, covered over with tea towels to keep them fresh.

'I can eat it,' said Alfie, who liked to be helpful.

'Ha,' said Margie. 'I'm sure you can. You're a bottomless pit, Alfie Summerfield. I don't know where you put it all. Honest, I don't.'

When Alfie's dad, Georgie, came home from

work at lunch time that day, he had a worried expression on his face. He didn't go out to the back yard to wash up like he usually did, even though he smelled a bit like milk and a bit like a horse. Instead, he stood in the front parlour reading a newspaper before folding it in half, hiding it under one of the sofa cushions and coming into the kitchen.

'All right, Margie,' he said, pecking his wife on the cheek.

'All right, Georgie.'

'All right, Alfie,' he said, tousling the boy's hair.

'All right, Dad.'

'Happy birthday, son. What age are you now anyway, twenty-seven?'

'I'm *five*,' said Alfie, who couldn't imagine what it would be like to be twenty-seven but felt very grown up to think that he was five at last.

'Five. I see,' said Georgie, scratching his chin. 'Seems like you've been around here a lot longer than that.'

'Out! Out! Out!' shouted Margie, waving her hands to usher them back into the front parlour. Alfie's mum always said there was nothing that annoyed her more than having her two men under her feet when she was trying to cook. And so Georgie and Alfie did what they were told, playing a game of Snakes and Ladders at the table by the window as they waited for the party to begin.

'Dad,' said Alfie.

'Yes, son?'

'How was Mr Asquith today?'

'Much better.'

'Did the vet take a look at him?'

'He did, yes. Whatever was wrong with him seems to have worked its way out of his system.'

Mr Asquith was Georgie's horse. Or rather, he was the dairy's horse; the one who pulled Georgie's milk float every morning when he was delivering the milk. Alfie had named him the day he'd been assigned to Georgie a year before; he'd heard the name so often on the wireless that it seemed it could only belong to someone very important and so decided it was just right for a horse.

'Did you give him a pat for me, Dad?'

'I did, son,' said Georgie.

Alfie smiled. He loved Mr Asquith. He absolutely loved him.

'Dad,' said Alfie a moment later.

'Yes, son?'

'Can I come to work with you tomorrow?'

Georgie shook his head. 'Sorry, Alfie. You're still too young for the milk float. It's more dangerous than you realize.'

'But you said that I could when I was older.'

'And when you're older, you can.'

'But I'm older now,' said Alfie. 'I could help all

our neighbours when they come to fill their milk jugs at the float.'

'It's more than my job's worth, Alfie.'

'Well, I could keep Mr Asquith company while you filled them yourself.'

'Sorry, son,' said Georgie. 'But you're still not old enough.'

Alfie sighed. There was nothing in the world he wanted more than to ride the milk float with his dad and help deliver the milk every morning, feeding lumps of sugar to Mr Asquith between streets, even though it meant getting up in the middle of the night. The idea of being out in the streets and seeing the city when everyone else was still in bed sent a shiver down his spine. And being his dad's right-hand man? What could be better? He'd asked whether he could do it at least a thousand times, but every time he asked, the answer was always the same: *Not yet, Alfie, you're still too young.*

'Do you remember when you were five?' asked Alfie.

'I do, son. That was the year my old man died. That was a rough year.'

'How did he die?'

'Down the mines.'

Alfie thought about it. He only knew one person who had died. Kalena's mother, Mrs Janáček, who had passed away from tuberculosis. Alfie could spell that word. *T-u-b-e-r-c-u-l-o-s-i-s.*

'What happened then?' he asked.

'When?'

'When your dad died.'

Georgie thought about it for a moment and shrugged his shoulders. 'Well, we moved to London, didn't we?' he said. 'Your Granny Summerfield said there was nothing in Newcastle for us any more. She said if we came here we could make a fresh start. She said I was the man of the house now.' He threw a five and a six, landed on blue 37 and slid down a snake all the way to white 19. 'Just my luck,' he said.

'You'll be able to stay up late tonight, won't you?' Alfie asked, and his dad nodded.

'Just for you, I will,' he said. 'Since it's your birthday, I'll stay up till nine. How does that sound?'

Alfie smiled; Georgie never went to bed any later than seven o'clock at night because of his early starts. 'I'm no good without my beauty sleep,' he always said, which made Margie laugh, and then he would turn to Alfie and say, 'Your mum only agreed to marry me on account of my good looks. But if I don't get a decent night's sleep I get dark bags under my eyes and my face grows white as a ghost and she'll run off with the postman.'

'I ran off with a milkman, and much good it did me,' Margie always said in reply, but she didn't mean it, because then they'd look at each other and smile, and sometimes she would yawn and say that she fancied an early night too, and up they'd go to bed, which meant Alfie had to go to bed too and this proved one thing to him: that yawning was contagious.

Despite the disappointing turn-out for his birthday party, Alfie tried not to mind too much. He knew that something was going on out there in the real world, something that all the adults were talking about, but it seemed boring and he wasn't really interested anyway. There'd been talk about it for months; the grown-ups were forever saying that something big was just round the corner, something that was going to affect them all. Sometimes Georgie would tell Margie that it was going to start any day now and they'd have to be ready for it, and sometimes, when she got upset, he said that she had nothing to worry about, that everything would turn out tickety-boo in the end, and that Europe was far too civilized to start a scrap that no one could possibly hope to win.

When the party started, everyone tried to be cheerful and pretend that it was a day just like any other. They played Hot Potato, where everyone sat in a circle and passed a hot potato to the next person and the first to drop it was out. (Kalena won that game.) Old Bill Hemperton set up a game of Penny Pitch in the front parlour, and Alfie came away three farthings the richer. Granny

Summerfield handed everyone a clothes peg and placed an empty milk bottle on the floor. Whoever could drop the peg into the bottle from the highest was the winner. (Margie was twice as good as everyone else at this.) But soon the adults stopped talking to the children and huddled together in corners with glum expressions on their faces while Alfie and Kalena listened in to their conversations and tried to understand what they were talking about.

'You're better off signing up now before they call you,' Old Bill Hemperton said. 'It'll go easier on you in the end, you mark my words.'

'Be quiet, you,' snapped Granny Summerfield, who lived in the house opposite Old Bill at number eleven and had never got along with him because he played his gramophone every morning with the windows open. She was a short, round woman who always wore a hairnet and kept her sleeves rolled up as if she was just about to go to work. 'Georgie's not signing up for anything.'

'Might not have a choice, Mum,' said Georgie, shaking his head.

'Shush – not in front of Alfie,' said Margie, tugging him on his arm.

'I'm just saying that this thing could run and run for years. I might have a better chance if I volunteer.'

'No, it'll all be over by Christmas,' said Mr

Janáček, whose black leather shoes were so shiny that almost everyone had remarked upon them. 'That's what everyone is saying.'

'Shush – not in front of Alfie,' said Margie again, raising her voice now.

'We're finished, we're all finished!' cried Granny Summerfield, taking her enormous handkerchief from her pocket and blowing her nose so loudly into it that Alfie burst out laughing. Margie didn't find it so funny though; she started to cry and ran out of the room, and Georgie ran after her.

More than four years had passed since that day, but Alfie still thought about it all the time. He was nine years old now and hadn't had any birthday parties in the years in between. But when he was going to sleep at night, he did his best to put together all the things he could remember about his family before they'd changed, because if he remembered them the way they used to be, then there was always the chance that one day they could be that way again.

Georgie and Margie had been very old when they got married – he knew that much. His dad had been almost twenty-one and his mum was only a year younger. Alfie found it hard to imagine what it would be like to be twenty-one years old. He thought that it would be difficult to hear things and that your sight would be a little fuzzy. He thought you wouldn't be able to get up out of the broken armchair in front of the fireplace without groaning and saying, *Well, that's me turning in for the night, then.* He guessed that the most important things in the world to you would be a nice cup of tea, a comfortable pair of slippers and a cosy cardigan. Sometimes, when he thought about it, he knew that one day he would be twenty-one years old too, but it seemed so far in the future that it was hard to imagine. He'd taken a piece of paper and pen once and written the numbers down, and realized that it would be 1930 before he was that age. 1930! That was centuries away. All right, maybe not centuries, but that's the way Alfie thought about it.

Alfie's fifth birthday party was both a happy and a sad memory. It was happy because he'd received some good presents: a set of eighteen different-coloured crayons and a sketchbook from his parents; a second-hand copy of *The Life and Strange Surprising Adventures of Robinson Crusoe* from Mr Janáček, who said that it would probably be too difficult for him now but that he'd be able to read it one day; a bag of sherbet lemons from Kalena. And he didn't mind that some of the presents were boring: a pair of socks from Granny Summerfield and a map of Australia from Old Bill Hemperton, who said that someday he might want to go down under, and if that day ever came, then this map was sure to come in handy.

'See there?' said Old Bill, pointing at a spot near the top of the map, where the green of the edges turned brown in the centre. 'That's where I'm from. A town called Mareeba. Finest little town in all of Australia. Ant hills the size of houses. If you ever go there, Alfie, you tell them Old Bill Hemperton sent you and they'll treat you like one of their own. I'm a hero back there on account of my connections.'

'What connections?' he asked, but Old Bill only winked and shook his head.

Alfie didn't know what to make of this, but in the days that followed he pinned the map to his bedroom wall anyway, he wore the socks that Granny Summerfield had given him, he used most of the colouring pencils and all of the sketchbook, he tried to read *Robinson Crusoe* but struggled with it (although he put it on his shelf to come back to when he was older) and he shared the sherbet lemons with Kalena.

These were the good memories.

The sad ones existed because that was when everything had changed. All the men from Damley Road had gathered outside on the street as the sun went down, their shirtsleeves rolled up, tugging at their braces as they spoke about things they called 'duty' and 'responsibility', taking little puffs of their cigarettes before pinching the tips closed again and putting the butts back in their waistcoat pockets for later on. Georgie had got into an argument with his oldest and closest friend, Joe Patience, who lived at number sixteen, about what they called the rights and wrongs of it all. Joe and Georgie had been friends since Georgie and Granny Summerfield moved to Damley Road – Granny Summerfield said that Joe had practically grown up in her kitchen – and had never exchanged a cross word until that afternoon. It was the day when Charlie Slipton, the paper boy from number twenty-one, who'd once thrown a stone at Alfie's head for no reason whatsoever, had come up and down the street six times with later and later editions of the newspaper, and managed to sell them all without even trying. And it was the day that had ended with Alfie's mum sitting in the broken armchair in front of the fireplace, sobbing as if the end of the world was upon them.

'Come on, Margie,' Georgie said, standing behind her and rubbing her neck. 'There's nothing to cry about, is there? Remember what everyone said – it'll all be over by Christmas. I'll be back here in time to help stuff the goose.'

'And you believe that, do you?' Margie said, looking up at him, her eyes red-rimmed with tears. 'You believe what they tell you?'

'What else can we do but believe?' said Georgie. 'We have to hope for the best.'

'Promise me, Georgie Summerfield,' said Margie. 'Promise me you won't sign up.'

There was a long pause before Alfie's dad spoke again. 'You heard what Old Bill said, love. It might be easier on me in the long term if—'

'And what about me? And Alfie? Will it be easier on us? Promise me, Georgie!'

'All right, love. Let's just see what happens, shall we? All them politicians might wake up tomorrow morning and change their minds about the whole thing anyway. We could be worrying over nothing.'

Alfie wasn't supposed to eavesdrop on his parents' private conversations – this was something that had got him into trouble once or twice in the past – but that night, the night he turned five, he sat on the staircase where he knew they couldn't see him and stared at his toes as he listened in. He hadn't intended sitting there for quite so long – he had only come down for a glass of water and a bit of leftover tongue that he'd had his eye on – but their conversation sounded so serious that it seemed like it might be a mistake to walk away from it. He gave a deep, resounding yawn – it had been a very long day, after all, as birthdays always are – and closed his eyes for a moment, laid his head on the step behind him, and before he knew it he was having a dream where someone was lifting him up and carrying him to a warm, comfortable place, and the next thing he knew he was opening his eyes again, only to find himself lying in his own little bed with the sun pouring through the thin curtains – the ones with the pale yellow flowers on them that Alfie said were meant for a girl's room, not a boy's.

The morning after his fifth birthday party, Alfie came downstairs to find his mother in her wash-day clothes with her hair tied up on her head, boiling water in every pot on the range, looking just as unhappy as she had the night before, and not just the normal unhappiness she felt every wash-day, which usually lasted from seven in the morning until seven at night. She looked up when she saw him but didn't seem to recognize him for a moment; when she did, she just offered him a dejected smile.

'Alfie,' she said. 'I thought I'd let you sleep in. You had a big day yesterday. Bring your sheets down to me, will you? There's a good boy.'

'Where's Dad?' asked Alfie.

'He's gone out.'

'Gone out where?'

'Oh, I don't know,' she said, unable to look him in the eye. 'You know your dad never tells me anything.'

Which Alfie knew wasn't true, because every

afternoon when his father came home from the dairy, he told Margie every single detail of his day from start to finish, and they sat there laughing while he explained how Bonzo Daly had left half a dozen churns outside in the yard without the lids on and the birds had got at them and spoiled the milk. Or how Petey Staples had cheeked the boss and been told that if he continued to complain he could just go and find another job where they put up with guff like that. Or how Mr Asquith had done the poo to end all poos outside Mrs Fairfax from number four's house and her a direct descendant (she claimed) of the last Plantagenet King of England and meant for better places than Damley Road. If Alfie knew one thing about his father, it was that he told his mother *everything*.

An hour later, he was sitting in the front parlour drawing in his new sketchbook while Margie took a rest from the washing, and Granny Summerfield, who'd come round for what she called a bit of a gossip – although it was really to bring her sheets for Margie to wash too – held the newspaper up to her face and squinted at the print, complaining over and over about why they made it so small.

'I can't read it, Margie,' she was saying. 'Are they trying to drive us all blind? Is that their plan?'

'Do you think Dad will take me on the float with him tomorrow?' asked Alfie.

'Did you ask him?'

'Yes, but he said I couldn't until I was older.'

'Well, then,' said Margie.

'But I'll be older tomorrow than I was yesterday,' said Alfie.

Before Margie could answer, the door opened, and to Alfie's astonishment a soldier marched in. He was tall and well built, the same size and shape as Alfie's dad, but he looked a little sheepish as he glanced around the room. Alfie couldn't help but be impressed by the uniform: a khaki-coloured jacket with five brass buttons down the centre, a pair of shoulder straps, trousers that tucked into knee socks, and big black boots. But why would a soldier just walk into their living room? he wondered. He hadn't even knocked on the front door! But then the soldier took his hat off and placed it under his arm, and Alfie realized that this wasn't just any soldier and it wasn't a stranger either.

It was Georgie Summerfield.

It was his dad.

And that was when Margie dropped her knitting on the floor, put both hands to her mouth and held them there for a few moments before running from the room and up the stairs while Georgie looked round at his son and mother and shrugged his shoulders.

'I had to,' he said finally. 'You can see that, Mum, can't you? I had to.'

'We're finished,' said Granny Summerfield, putting the newspaper down and turning away from her son as she looked out of the window, where more young men were walking through their own front doors wearing uniforms just like Georgie's. 'We're all finished.'

And that was everything that Alfie remembered about turning five.

2

IF YOU WERE THE ONLY BOCHE IN THE TRENCH

The Janáčeks had already been gone for almost two years when Alfie stole the shoeshine box.

They had lived three doors down from the Summerfields for as long as he could remember, and Kalena, who was six weeks older than him, had been his best friend since they were babies. Whenever Alfie was in her house in the evening, Mr Janáček could be found sitting at the kitchen table with the shoeshine box laid out before him, shining his shoes for the next day.

'I believe a man should always present himself to the world with elegance and grace,' he told Alfie. 'It is what marks us out from the animals.'

All the people on Damley Road were friends, or they had been before the war began. There were twelve terraced houses on either side of the street, each one attached to the next by a thin wall that carried muffled conversations through to the neighbours. Some of the houses had window boxes outside, some didn't, but everyone made an effort to keep the place tidy. Alfie and Kalena lived on the side with all the even numbers; Granny Summerfield lived opposite, with all the odd ones, which Margie said was particularly appropriate. Each house had one window facing onto the street from the front parlour, with two more up top, and every door was painted the same colour: yellow. Alfie remembered the day Joe Patience, the conchie from number sixteen, painted his door red, and all the women came out on the street to watch him, shaking their heads and whispering to each other in outrage. Joe was political – everyone knew that. Old Bill said he was 'his own man', whatever that meant. He was out on strike more often than he was at work and was forever handing out leaflets about workers' rights. He said that women should have the vote, and not even all the women agreed with him about that. (Granny Summerfield said she'd rather have the plague.) He owned a beautiful old clarinet too, and sometimes he sat outside his front door playing it; when he did, Helena Morris from number eighteen would stand in her doorway and stare down the street at him until her mother came out and told her to stop making a show of herself.

Alfie liked Joe Patience, and he thought it was funny that his name seemed to be the opposite of his character because he was always getting worked up over something. After he painted his front door red, three of the men, Mr Welton from number five, Mr Jones from number nineteen and Georgie Summerfield, Alfie's dad, went over to have a word with him about it. Georgie didn't want to go but the two men insisted, since he was Joe's oldest friend.

'It's not on, Joe,' said Mr Jones as all the women came out on the street and pretended to wash their windows.

'Why not?'

'Well, take a look around you. It's out of place.'

'Red is the colour of the working man! And we're all working men here, aren't we?'

'We have yellow doors here on Damley Road,' said Mr Welton.

'Whoever said they had to be yellow?'

'That's just the way things have always been. You don't want to go mucking about with traditional ways.'

'Then how will things ever get better?' asked Joe, raising his voice even though the three men were standing directly in front of him. 'For pity's sake, it's just a door! What does it matter what colour it is?'

'Maybe Joe's right,' said Georgie, trying to calm everyone's tempers. 'It's not that important, is it? As long as the paint isn't chipping off and letting the street down.'

'I might have known you'd be on his side,' said Mr Jones, sneering at him even though it had been his idea to ask Georgie to join them in the first place. 'Old pals together, eh?'

'Yes,' said Georgie with a shrug, as if it was the most natural thing in the world. 'Old pals together. What's wrong with that?'

In the end, there was nothing that Mr Welton or Mr Jones could do about the red door, and it stayed that way until the following summer, when Joe decided to change it again and painted it green in support of the Irish – who, Joe said, were doing all they could to break off the shackles of their imperial overlords. Alfie's dad just laughed and said that if he wanted to waste his money on paint, then it was nothing to do with him. Granny Summerfield said that if Joe's mother was still alive, she'd be ashamed.

'Oh, I don't know,' said Margie. 'He has an independent streak, that's all. I quite like that about him.'

'He's not a bad fellow, Joe Patience,' agreed Georgie.

'He's his own man,' repeated Old Bill Hemperton.

'He's lovely looking, despite everything,' said Margie. 'Helena Morris is sweet on him.'

'She'd be ashamed,' insisted Granny Summerfield.

But other than that, the people on Damley Road always seemed to get along very well. They were neighbours and friends. And no one seemed more a part of that community than Kalena and her father.

Mr Janáček ran the sweet shop at the end of the road. It wasn't just a sweet shop, of course – he also sold newspapers, string, notepads, pencils, birthday cards, apples, catapults, footballs, laces, boot polish, carbolic soap, tea, screwdrivers, purses, shoehorns and light bulbs – but as far as Alfie was concerned the most important thing he sold was sweets, so he called it the sweet shop. Behind the counter stood rows of tall clear glass containers crammed full of sherbet lemons, apple and pear drops, bull's-eyes, liquorice sticks and caramel surprises, and whenever Alfie had a penny or two to spare he always went straight to Mr Janáček, who let him stand there for as long as he liked while he made up his mind.

'Sometimes, Alfie,' he said, leaning over the counter and taking off his spectacles to clean them, 'I think that you enjoy deciding what to spend your pennies on more than you do eating the sweets themselves.'

Mr Janáček had a funny voice because he wasn't English. He was from Prague, but had come to London ten years before and had never lost his accent. *What* came out as *Vat. Sweets* as *sveets.* Kalena didn't speak like him because she'd been born in their house at number six and had never been outside London in her life.

'You're the luckiest person I know,' Alfie told her one day as they sat together on the edge of the pavement, chewing on a liquorice allsort and watching the coal man deliver a bag into Mrs Scutworth's at number fifteen. The coal man's face and hands were completely black with soot, but he must have just rolled up his sleeves before he arrived because his forearms were pale white.

'Why do you say that?' asked Kalena, carefully peeling the skin off a banana.

'Because your dad runs a sweet shop,' he replied as if it was the most obvious thing in the world. 'There isn't *any* job in the world that's better than that. Except maybe working on the milk float.'

Kalena shook her head. 'There's *lots* of jobs better than that,' she said. 'I'm not going to run a sweet shop when I grow up.'

'Then what will you do?' asked Alfie, frowning.

'I'm going to be Prime Minister,' said Kalena.

Alfie didn't know what to say to that but he thought it sounded very impressive. When he told his parents over tea that night, they both burst out laughing.

'Kalena Janáček? The Prime Minister?' said

Georgie, shaking his head. 'I've heard everything now. Pass me the carrots, love.'

'A Prime Minister's wife, more like,' said Margie, reaching for the dish.

'Well, I'd vote for her,' said Alfie, defending his friend. He didn't like the way they thought this was so funny.

'You'd be the only one,' said Georgie. 'She wouldn't even be able to vote for herself, so how she thinks she can get the top job is beyond me. Bit chewy, these carrots, aren't they?'

'Why can't she vote for herself?' asked Alfie.

'Women can't vote, Alfie,' said Margie, cutting another slice of beef from the roast and putting it on his plate with an extra potato. (This was in the days when they were able to eat things like beef and potatoes for tea. Before the war broke out.)

'Why not?'

'It's the way things have always been.'

'But why?'

'Is a letter that comes between x and z,' said Margie. 'Now eat your tea, Alfie, and stop asking so many questions. And there's nothing wrong with them carrots, Georgie Summerfield, so mind you eat them up too. I don't spend my afternoons cooking just to clear away a plate of leftovers.'

Alfie didn't think any of these answers explained anything, but he thought it was a good thing that Kalena was ambitious. Later that night, he lay in bed and thought about all the things he could do when he grew up. He could be a train driver. Or a policeman. He could be a school-teacher or a fireman. He could go to work on the milk float with his dad or be a bus conductor like Mr Welton. He could be an explorer like Ernest Shackleton, who was always in the papers these days. They all seemed like good jobs – but then inspiration struck and he nearly jumped out of bed in excitement.

The following afternoon, he marched into Mr Janáček's sweet shop and waited until Mr Candlemas from number thirteen had counted out a handful of change for his tobacco before sitting down on the high stool next to the counter and staring up at the jars of sweets.

'Hello, Alfie,' said Mr Janáček.

'Hello, Mr Janáček,' said Alfie.

'What will it be today, then?' *Vat vill it be today, zen?*

Alfie shook his head. 'Nothing, thanks,' he said. 'I've no pocket money till Monday. I wanted to ask you a question, that's all.'

Mr Janáček nodded and came over to stand next to the boy, shrugging his shoulders. 'Ask me anything you want.' *Anysing you vant.*

'Well, you're not getting any younger, are you, Mr Janáček?' said Alfie. This was a phrase he'd overheard Old Bill Hemperton say. Whenever he was asked to do anything to help out on the street, he said he couldn't, that whatever it was was a young man's game and that he wasn't getting any younger.

Mr Janáček laughed. 'How old do you think I am, Alfie?'

Alfie thought about it. He knew from experience – after a particularly unpleasant conversation with Mrs Tamorin from number twenty – that it was always best to guess younger than you really thought. 'Sixty?' he said, hoping that he might be right. (He really thought that Mr Janáček was about seventy-five.)

Mr Janáček laughed and shook his head. 'Close,' he said. 'I'm twenty-nine. Only a few years older than your father.'

Alfie didn't believe him for a moment but he let it go.

'Well, one day you'll be too old to run the shop, won't you?' he asked.

'I suppose so,' he said. 'Although not for a long time, I hope.'

'Because I was talking to Kalena,' continued Alfie. 'And she said that she won't work here when she's grown up on account of the fact that she's planning on becoming Prime Minister. And I thought that you'll probably need someone else to help out then, won't you? When you can't move around like you used to and you're not able to reach up for the things on the top shelves.'

Mr Janáček considered this. 'Perhaps,' he said. 'But why do you ask, Alfie? Are you applying for the position?'

Alfie thought about it. He wasn't sure if he wanted to commit himself fully. 'I just think you might keep me in mind, that's all,' he said. 'I'm a hard worker, I'm honest and I love sweets.'

'But we don't just sell sweets, do we? You'd have to like everything else too.'

'I can't imagine getting too excited about string or candles,' said Alfie. 'But I'd do my best. And in the meantime, I could take over every week when you have your day off.'

Mr Janáček raised an eyebrow. 'What day do I have off?' he asked in surprise. 'I work, I work and I work. I have no rest!'

'But you always close on Friday evenings and don't open again until Sunday morning,' said Alfie.

'Ah, but that is not a day off,' said Mr Janáček. 'That is Shabbat. The Jewish day of rest. There are blessings to be made on Friday night: Kalena lights our candles, prayers are offered. We do not work but we keep busy. I could not open the shop on this day. But your offer is a generous one, Alfie, and be assured that I will keep you in mind when it is time for me to retire.'

Alfie smiled. That was good enough for him. He

looked over behind Mr Janáček at the flag that was pinned to the wall beside the cash register. It was quite complicated, with a red stripe across the top, a white one in the centre, and red and green squares underneath. Two crowns stood side by side over two emblems.

'What's that?' asked Alfie.

Mr Janáček glanced over to see what the boy was looking at. 'Why, it's a flag,' he said.

'It's not a flag of England.'

'No, it's the flag of my homeland. Where I was born and where I grew up. Prague is a very beautiful city,' he added, stroking his chin and staring off into the lemon twisters. 'Perhaps the most beautiful in the world. The city of Mozart and Dvořák. The city where *Figaro* and *Don Giovanni* were first performed. And if you have not crossed the Charles Bridge over the Vltava as the sun drops behind the castle, then you have not lived, my friend. You will visit it one day, I am sure of it.'

Alfie frowned. He had understood almost nothing of what Mr Janáček had just said.

'If Prague is so wonderful,' he asked, 'then why did you move to London?'

Mr Janáček's face burst into a wide smile and he looked as happy as Alfie had ever seen him. 'For the best reason in the world,' he explained. 'For love.'

Alfie jumped off the stool then, said his

goodbyes and marched back outside. He had no interest in hearing about this. Love was something that grown-ups talked about and girls read about – although Kalena never discussed it; she said she couldn't let herself be distracted by love or she might never become Prime Minister – but that Alfie had no interest in at all. He could tell that Mrs Janáček was very pretty, for an old woman anyway, but he couldn't imagine that he could ever fall in love with her.

Of course, Mrs Janáček had died in 1913, the year before the war began. She got very sick and very thin, and soon she couldn't leave the house. Margie went to call on her every day, and Alfie overheard her telling Georgie that she was 'wasting away, poor woman', and soon she was gone and Mr Janáček and Kalena were left alone. Alfie tried to talk to his friend about what had happened but she said she didn't want to discuss it, not just yet, so instead he simply took her out to play every day, even when she didn't want to go. He told her all his worst jokes, one of which, three months after her mother died, made her laugh out loud, and everything seemed to be all right again after that.

Alfie hadn't seen the Janáčeks since the spring of 1915. By then, the newspapers were talking about the war all the time and a lot of the men from

Damley Road, including Alfie's dad, Georgie, were either training to be soldiers or were already fighting in Belgium or northern France. Some were too young yet but kept saying that they would sign up the minute they turned eighteen. Others were keeping their heads down and not talking about it at all because they didn't want to go.

Even Leonard Hopkins from number two, who everyone knew had a shoeshine stand at King's Cross and almost never went to school, spending every penny he earned on girls and hair tonic, had signed up, and he had only just turned sixteen.

'They didn't ask any questions, that's what I heard,' Granny Summerfield confided in Margie while Alfie was eating his tea one evening. 'But then, those recruiting sergeants don't care, do they? They'll take any lamb to the slaughter. Leonard hasn't even started shaving yet. It's a disgrace, if you ask me.'

And then there was Joe Patience, the conchie from number sixteen – he wasn't a conchie yet, of course – who said that the whole thing was a nonsense: it was just about land and money and giving more to the rich and keeping the poor in their place, and he didn't care what anyone said or did, he'd never lift a gun, he'd never wear a uniform and he'd never wanted to see France anyway so he didn't care if he never did.

A lot of people got angry with Joe Patience, but

back then, in 1915, they didn't do anything more than shout at him when he started talking politics. It wasn't until later that they did worse things.

That February, the same day that Alfie got a letter from his dad telling him all about the training barracks at Aldershot, Margie called him into the kitchen where she was counting out change from her purse. Back then, she was still at home most of the time where she was knitting from morning till night, as were most of the women from Damley Road, and sending socks and jumpers over to the men at something she called 'the Front'.

'Run down to Mr Janáček for me, will you, Alfie?' she asked. 'I need a couple of apples, a bag of flour, and today's newspaper. Make sure it's the latest edition. There'll be a penny left over for a few sweets.'

Alfie's face lit up as he grabbed the money and ran down the street to where Mr Janáček was standing outside his shop staring, trembling a little, his face pale. The windows had been smashed, there was glass everywhere on the road, and someone had scrawled three words in paint all over the front door: *No Spies Here!*

'Who's a spy?' asked Alfie, frowning. 'And what happened to your windows? And do you have any apple drops in stock?'

Mr Janáček, who was always so friendly, stared down at him but didn't smile. His shoes were as shiny as ever. 'What do you need, Alfie?' he asked in a voice trembling with rage and fear.

'A couple of apples, a bag of flour and today's newspaper. I'm supposed to make sure it's the latest edition.'

'You better go to the corner shop at Damley Park,' said Mr Janáček. 'I don't think I'll be open for business today. As you can see, my windows have all been broken.' *My vindows have all been broken.*

'Who did this?' asked Alfie, feeling the soft crunch of the glass beneath his shoes.

'I said go to Damley Park,' said Mr Janáček, raising his voice a little. 'I don't have time for this right now.'

Alfie sighed and turned away. He hated going to Mrs Bessworth's shop as she had a reputation for stealing children, baking them in pies and eating them for her tea. (A friend of Alfie's knew somebody whose cousin had a neighbour who this had happened to so it was definitely true.)

This wasn't the last time that the shop windows were smashed, but every time it happened Mr Janáček replaced them within a day or two. And then, one evening, as Kalena was playing hopscotch on the street, the squares marked off in chalk on the pavement, and Alfie was sitting on the kerb watching her, an army van appeared and pulled up outside number six; when Mr Janáček opened the door they told him that he was to come with them immediately or there'd be trouble.

'But I have done nothing wrong!' he protested.

'You're a German,' shouted Mrs Milchin from number seven, whose two oldest boys had already been killed at Ypres and whose youngest son, Johnny, was about to turn eighteen. (No one had seen Johnny in weeks; the rumour was that Mrs Milchin had sent him to her sister-in-law in the Outer Hebrides.)

'But I'm not!' protested Mr Janáček. 'I am from Prague. You are aware of this!' *You are avare of zis!* 'I have never even been to Germany!'

Kalena ran to her father and he threw his arms around her. 'You're not taking us,' he shouted.

'Come on now,' said the army men. 'It'll be easier for you if you come peacefully.'

'That's right, take him away. He's a spy!' shouted Mrs Milchin, and now Margie was out on the street too, looking aghast at what was taking place.

'Leave him be,' she shouted, running down and jumping in between the Janáčeks and the soldiers. 'He just told you that he's not German, and anyway, he's lived here for years. Kalena was born on this street. They're no threat to anyone.'

'Step aside, Mrs,' said the army man, signalling to one of his colleagues to open the back doors of the van.

'You're a traitor, Margie Summerfield!' cried

Mrs Milchin. 'Cosying up to the enemy! You ought to be ashamed!'

'But he hasn't done anything! My husband's a soldier,' she added, as if this would help.

'Step aside, Mrs,' repeated the army man, 'or you'll be taken into custody too.'

A lot of fighting happened then, and it took almost twenty minutes for the Janáčeks to be loaded into the van. They weren't allowed to go back into their house or to take anything with them. Mr Janáček pleaded to be permitted to take a picture of his wife, but he was told that they could take the clothes they were standing up in and nothing else. Kalena ran to Alfie's mum and threw her arms around her, and one of the soldiers had to drag her away as the little girl screamed and wept. The last Alfie saw of them was Mr Janáček weeping in the back of the van while Kalena stared out of the window behind her at Alfie, waving silently. She looked very brave, and Alfie knew there and then that she *would* become Prime Minister one day, and when she did, she would make sure that nothing like this ever happened again.

Later that night, Margie explained what had happened. '*Persons of special interest,* that's what they call them,' she told him. 'Anyone German. Anyone Russian. Anyone from the Austro-Hungarian Empire, if I have it right. And that's where the Janáčeks come from. Maybe it's for the best.'

'But it's not fair,' said Alfie.

'No, but they'll be kept safe while the war is on. A few months on the Isle of Man, it's not so bad when you think about it. Think of all the damage that has been done to their shop, after all. It was only a matter of time before those vandals turned their attentions to Mr Janáček himself.'

The house at number six had remained empty ever since. No one else came to live there and no one ever went inside. Until one day, when Margie was sitting in the front room counting the pennies from her purse and deciding whether she should pay the rent, the coal man or the grocer that week – it couldn't possibly be all three; it probably couldn't even be two – Alfie had an idea.

He ran out of the back door and made his way down the ginnel towards number six, jumped over the wall into the Janáčeks' back yard and broke the kitchen window with a stone he found near the door. Reaching in, he opened the latch and pulled it up, climbed inside and looked around, searching for the one thing that he thought might save his family from homelessness or starvation.

He found it in the corner of the parlour, sitting on the floor next to a rocking chair.

Mr Janáček's shoeshine box.

When Alfie left, it was the only thing he took with him.

3

KEEP THE HOME FIRES BURNING

They said it would be over by Christmas, but four Christmases had already come and gone, a fifth was on the way, and the war showed no sign of coming to an end.

Alfie was nine years old now, and six mornings a week, his mum shook him awake when she was leaving for work. He still got a shock when he opened his eyes to see her standing there in the half-light, the white dress uniform of a Queen's Nurse gathered close around her neck and waist, the pleated cap settled neatly on her head as her tight blonde curls peeped out from underneath.

'Alfie,' she said, her face pale and tired from another night with so little sleep. 'Alfie, wake up. It's six o'clock.'

He groaned and rolled over, pulling the scratchy blanket over his head even though it meant his feet would stick out the other end, and tried to go back to sleep. He'd asked Margie for a new blanket, a longer and heavier one, but she said they couldn't afford one, that times were too tough now for unnecessary expenses. Alfie had been having a dream where he set sail for North Africa but his ship was destroyed in a storm. He'd managed to swim to a deserted island, where he was living off coconuts and fish and having any number of adventures. He always had this dream whenever he read *Robinson Crusoe*, and he was halfway through it again, for the fourth time. He'd stopped reading the night before just as Crusoe and Friday were watching the cannibals arrive in canoes with three prisoners ready for the pot. A big fight was about to break out; it was one of his favourite parts.

'Alfie, I don't have time for this,' said Margie. 'Wake up. I can't leave the house until you're out of bed.'

Her voice was unforgiving; one thing that Alfie noticed about the way his mother had changed over the last four years was how harsh she'd become. She never played with him any more – she was always too tired for that. She didn't read to him before bed; she couldn't, as she had to be back in the hospital by eight o'clock for the night shift. She talked about money all the time, or the lack of it. And she shouted at him for no reason and then looked as if she wanted to burst into tears for losing her temper.

'Alfie, please,' she said, pulling the sheets back so the cold got to him. 'You have to get up. Can't you just do this one thing for me?'

He knew he didn't have any choice, so he rolled over onto his back once again, opened his eyes, and gave a tremendous yawn and stretch before climbing slowly out of bed. Only when his feet were both planted on the floor did Margie stand up straight and nod, satisfied.

'Finally,' she said. 'Honestly, Alfie, I don't know why we have to go through this palaver every day. You're nine years old now. A little co-operation is all I ask for. Now get some breakfast into you, have a wash and go to school. I'll be back around two o'clock so I'll cook us something nice for our tea. What do you fancy?'

'Sausages, beans and chips,' said Alfie.

'Chance would be a fine thing,' said Margie, making a laughing sound that wasn't really a laugh at all. (She didn't laugh very much any more. Not in the way she used to when she said she'd run off with the postman.) 'Tripe and onions, I'm afraid. That's all we can afford.'

Alfie wondered why she asked what he fancied when it didn't seem to matter what his answer was. Still, he felt pleased that she would already be home when he finished school. It was usually much later before she got back from work.

'We'll have a bit of tea together,' she said,

softening slightly. 'But I'm on a night shift again, I'm afraid, so you'll have to look after yourself this evening or you can pop over to Granny Summerfield's if you like. You won't get into any trouble, will you?'

Alfie shook his head. He'd tried talking her out of night shifts before but he never had any luck; she got a quarter extra in her pay packet when she worked after eight o'clock at night, and that quarter, she told him, could be the difference between them keeping a roof over their heads and not. He knew better than to bother trying any more. Margie stared at him for a moment, her hand reaching out and smoothing down his hair, and her expression changed a little. She didn't seem angry now. It was as if she was remembering the way things used to be. She sat down on the bed next to him and put her arm around his shoulders, and he cuddled into her, closing his eyes, feeling sleep returning.

After a moment he looked up and followed the direction of his mother's eyes until he found himself staring at the framed portrait of his father that stood on the table next to his bed. He wasn't wearing a soldier's uniform in it; instead he was standing in the yard at the dairy with a very young Alfie sitting on his shoulders, a big smile spread across his face, and Mr Asquith standing next to both of them, looking at the camera with an expression that suggested that this was an indignity he could do without. (Alfie always said that Mr Asquith was a very proud horse.) He couldn't remember when it had been taken but it had been standing on the table by his bed since the day Georgie had left for Aldershot Barracks four years earlier. Granny Summerfield had put it there that same evening.

'Oh Alfie,' said Margie, kissing him on his head as she stood up and made her way towards the door. 'I do my best for you. You know that, don't you?'

After she left for work, Alfie went downstairs, ran outside for the scoop that sat behind the back door, and filled it with ashes from the base of the kitchen range. Then he ran down to the privy at the end of the garden as quickly as he could, trying not to feel the ice in the air or spill any of the precious cinders. He hated going there first thing in the morning, particularly now, in late October, when it was still so dark and the air was so frosty, but there was no way around it.

It was freezing inside, seven different spiders and something that looked like an overfed beetle crawled over his feet as he sat there, he could hear the scurrying of rats behind the woodwork, and he groaned when he remembered that he'd forgotten the squares of yesterday's newspaper that he meticulously cut up every night before going to bed – but fortunately Margie had taken them outside earlier, pinned a hole through their centre and hung them from a piece of string off the hook, so he didn't need to go back indoors.

When he had finished his business, he poured the ashes down the toilet and hoped that the compost heap around the back of the out-house – the worst place he had ever seen in his entire life – would not get clogged up again. It had happened a few months before, and Margie had to pay the night-soil men two shillings to clear it all away; afterwards, uncertain whether they would have enough money for the rent, she had sat down in the broken armchair in front of the fireplace and cried her eyes out, whispering Georgie's name under her breath over and over again as if he might be able to come back and save them from possible eviction.

Alfie ran back inside, washed his hands and sat down at the kitchen table, where Margie had cut two slices of bread for him and left them on a plate next to a small scraping of butter and, to his astonishment, a tiny pot of jam with a muslin lid held in place by a piece of string. Alfie stared at it and blinked a couple of times. It had been months since he'd tasted jam. He picked it up and read the label. It was handwritten and contained only one word, written with a thick black pen.

Gooseberry.

Sometimes the parents of the soldiers in the hospital brought in a little something for the Queen's Nurses, and when they did, it was usually a treat like this: something they'd made themselves from the fruit they grew in their gardens or allotments. That must have been where Margie had got it. Alfie wondered whether his mother had eaten some herself or whether she'd kept it specially for him. He stood up and went over to the sink, where his mother's breakfast things were sitting, still unwashed, a small pool of cold brown tea sitting at the base of her mug. In the old days, before the war, Margie would never have left things like this; she would have rinsed them out and turned them upside down on the draining board for Georgie to dry later. He picked up the plate and examined it. There were a few crumbs on the side and a trace of condensation from where the heat of the toast had clashed with the coldness of the porcelain. He looked at the knife. It was almost clean. He gave it a sniff. It didn't smell of butter and there wasn't a trace of jam on it. If she'd used any, it would have left a bit behind.

She'd saved it all for him.

Alfie filled the kettle, put it on the range, threw a few sticks on top of the still-red embers inside and waited for the whistle before making himself a cup of tea. He always felt like a grown-up waiting for the leaves to brew. He didn't much like the taste of it, but it made him feel important to sit at the table in the morning with a steaming mug and a slice of toast before him, the newspaper propped up against the milk jug. It was how Georgie had always done things. Before he went away.

Charlie Slipton from number twenty-one didn't deliver the papers any more. He'd left for the war in 1917 and been killed a few months later. Alfie had written the name of the place where he died in his notebook but still couldn't pronounce it correctly. *Passchendaele.* Now the papers were delivered by Charlie's youngest brother, Jack, who had just turned ten and never spoke to anyone. Alfie had tried to make friends with him but eventually gave up when it became clear that he preferred to be left alone.

Looking at the newspaper now made him think of that horrible day a year ago when they'd heard about Charlie's death. It was a Sunday morning, so both he and Margie had been at home when there was a knock at the door. Margie, who had been baking bread, looked up in surprise, running the back of her hand against her forehead and leaving a white streak of flour behind. They didn't have many callers. Granny Summerfield had her own key and usually came straight in without so much as a by-your-leave. Old Bill next door always did a sort of *rat-a-tat-tat* on the woodwork so they'd know it was him. And of course Mr Janáček and Kalena had been taken away to the Isle of Man. Alfie didn't like to think about what had happened to them there.

'Who do you think that is?' asked Margie, rinsing her hands in the sink before walking into the hallway and standing before the door for a moment as if she might be able to see straight through to the other side. Alfie followed her, and after a moment she stepped forward, reached for the latch and opened it.

There were two men standing outside, both wearing military uniforms. One was quite old with a grey moustache, a pair of spectacles and dark blue eyes. He wore a very fine pair of leather gloves, which he was in the process of removing when the door was opened. The other man was much younger and had cut himself shaving that morning; Alfie could see a bead of blood clotted on his cheek. He had bright red hair that stuck out at all angles and looked as if it would put up a good fight against any brush that tried to tame it. Alfie stared at him in wonder. He'd never seen hair that red before, not even on Mr Carstairs, his teacher at Damley Road School, who everybody called 'Ginger' even though his hair was really more like a burned orange.

'Don't,' said Margie, holding onto the front door as she stared at the two men, her hand clutching the frame tightly. Alfie saw how white her knuckles became as she gripped it. '*Don't*,' she repeated, much louder this time, and Alfie frowned, wondering what she could possibly mean by this single word.

'Mrs Slipton?' said the older man, the one with the moustache, as the redhead stood to his full height and looked over Margie's shoulder to lock eyes with Alfie. His expression turned to one of sorrow when he saw the boy, and he bit his lip and looked away.

'What?' asked Margie, her voice rising in surprise at being addressed by the wrong name. Alfie stepped forward beside his mum now, and he noticed all the doors opening on the opposite side of the street and the women coming out and putting their hands to their faces. The curtain at number eleven twitched, and he could see Granny Summerfield staring out, her hands pressed to the side of her head. Mr Asquith trotted by with young Henry Lyons on the bench-seat. Henry couldn't fill a milk jug to save his life; everyone said so. He'd start pouring and half the churn would end up on the side of the road. But the dairy needed a delivery man, and Henry was deaf so couldn't go to war. Alfie was sure that Mr Asquith stared in his direction as he passed, looking over the boy's shoulder in search of his true master.

'Mrs Slipton, I'm Sergeant Malley,' said the

man. 'This is Lieutenant Hobton. May we come in for a moment?'

'No,' said Margie.

'Mrs Slipton, please,' he replied in a resigned tone, as if he was accustomed to this type of response. 'If we could just come in and sit down, then—'

'You've got the wrong house,' said Margie, her words catching in her throat, and she almost stumbled before putting her hand on Alfie's shoulder to steady herself. 'Oh my God, you've got the wrong house. How can you do that? This is number twelve. You want number twenty-one. You've got the numbers backwards.'

The older man stared at her for a moment; then his expression changed to one of utter dismay as the redhead pulled a piece of paper from his inside pocket and ran his eyes across it quickly.

'Sarge,' he said, holding the paper out and pointing at something.

The sergeant's lip curled up in fury and he glared at the younger man as if he wanted to hit him. 'What's wrong with you, Hobton?' he hissed. 'Can't you read? Can't you check before we knock on a door?' He turned back then and looked at Margie and Alfie, shaking his head. 'I'm sorry,' he said. 'I'm so very, very sorry.'

And with that the two men turned round but remained on the street, looking left and right, their eyes scanning the numbers on the doors before turning in the direction of Mr Janáček's sweet shop, where the windows were still boarded up from when they'd been smashed a couple of years before and the three words painted in white remained.

No Spies Here!

Margie stepped back into the hall, gasping, but Alfie stayed in the doorway. He watched as the two soldiers made their way slowly along the street. Every door was open now. And outside every door stood a wife or a mother. Some were crying. Some were praying. Some were shaking their heads, hoping that the men wouldn't stop before them. And every time Sergeant Malley and Lieutenant Hobton passed one of the houses, the woman at the door blessed herself and ran inside, slamming it behind her and putting the latch on in case the two men changed their minds and came back.

Finally they stopped at number twenty-one, where Charlie's mother, Mrs Slipton, was standing. Alfie couldn't hear what she was saying but he could see her crying, trying to push the soldiers away. She reached out with both hands and slapped Redhead across the face, but somehow he didn't seem to mind. The older man reached forward and whispered something to her, and then they went inside and stayed there, and Alfie found himself alone on the street again. Everyone else was indoors, counting their lucky stars that the two soldiers hadn't stopped at their door.

Later that day, Alfie heard that Charlie Slipton had been killed and he remembered the afternoon when Charlie had thrown a stone at his head for no reason whatsoever. He wasn't sure how he was supposed to feel. That was the thing about the war, he realized. It made everything so confusing.

Alfie didn't read much of the *Daily Mirror* but he liked to look at the headlines, and he picked it up now to see what was going on in the world. More news about the Marne; there was always something going on there. Details of casualties and fatalities from a place called Amiens. A report on a speech by the Prime Minister, Mr Lloyd George, who Alfie was sick of reading about because he gave speeches every day.

And then, finally, he did what he always did in the morning. He turned to page four to read the numbers. The number of deaths on our side. The number of deaths on their side. The number of wounded. The number missing in action. But there was only one number that Alfie really cared about: 14278. His dad's number. The number they'd assigned him when he signed up.

He ran his finger along the list.

14143, Smith, D., Royal Fusiliers
14275, Dempster, C. K., Gloucestershire Regiment

15496, Wallaby, A., Seaforth Highlanders
15700, Crosston, J., Sherwood Foresters (Notts & Derby Regiment)

He breathed a sigh of relief and put the paper down, sipping his tea, trying to think of something else. He shivered a little; the house was always cold. Margie put a few coals on the fire first thing in the morning but she said there was no point heating the whole place all day when there was just the two of them and she'd be at work and he'd be at school.

'Throwing money away, that is,' she said. 'No, we can live with the cold in the mornings. When you get home from school, you can light it for the evening. Only a few coals, mind, and not too many sticks. Kindling isn't cheap.'

Alfie finished his breakfast and went over to the sink, washing everything that was sitting there – Margie's breakfast things and his own. He dried them with the tea towel, then hung it on the hook next to the range before putting everything away in the cupboard. He took out the scissors and left them on top of the newspaper so he could cut it into squares later; today's news was tomorrow's toilet paper. He looked around and wondered whether the floor needed sweeping but it seemed clean enough. That was one of Alfie's jobs now; he kept the place shipshape and Bristol fashion. That's what Margie called it, anyway.

'We all have to pitch in,' she said. 'I wouldn't ask you if I had time to do it myself.'

Alfie didn't mind. He hated mess.

He put the kettle on the stove again and heated some more water, poured it in the sink and let the carbolic soap sit in it for a minute to soften. Then he took his pyjamas off and stood in the middle of the kitchen floor – he'd never have done this if Margie was home; he'd have told her to stay outside and put a chair against the door just in case she forgot – and gave himself a bit of a wash, upstairs and down. There was a second towel hanging by the fireplace and he used that to dry himself. It was rough against his skin and he hated the feel of it, but it was the only one they had. When he was done, he ran back upstairs and got dressed.

It was a Tuesday – a school day. But Alfie didn't go to school very much any more. The teachers didn't seem to mind. They didn't take a roll-call and they never called on anyone's mother to say that someone wasn't showing up. He went sometimes, of course, maybe twice a week. Usually on a Monday and a Thursday, because Monday was when they studied history and Alfie was very interested in history, especially anything to do with kings and queens and all the wars that had been fought for the crown of England; on Thursdays they did reading and Alfie was the best in the class at reading – he was the best in the school, in fact – and he loved to hear Mrs Jillson, the librarian, reading from a book in class or passing it around so that everyone could have a go at a page or two. Mrs Jillson was as old as the hills but she put on funny voices and made all the children do the same thing, and Alfie loved that part of it.

All the teachers now were different to the ones he'd had a few years before. Back then, there were a lot of young men in the school and they were good fun and always wanted a kick-about at lunch time. Now, of course, there wasn't a single young man left, except Mr Carstairs, who had two bad legs and walked with crutches. There was hardly a single young man anywhere, in fact, except for Joe Patience, the conchie from number sixteen, and no one ever talked to him. Not even Granny Summerfield, who'd known him since he was a child and had once said that he was like a second son to her – or that she was like a second mother to him: Alfie couldn't remember which. (Now you couldn't mention Joe's name to Granny Summerfield or she'd lose her temper, and once Alfie, watching from his window, had seen them passing in the street and Granny had slapped him, hard, across the face. Joe Patience! Who was the nicest, friendliest man you could possibly meet!)

The school was now run by old people, some of

whom used to be teachers before the war and who said that they thought they were finished with all this malarkey, that they'd been looking forward to a long and happy retirement. People like Mrs Jillson or Mr Flaker, the retired civil servant, or Mr Cratchley, whose son used to teach in the school but was 'over there' now, as he told them every day when he asked them to say a prayer for Cecil, for that was his son's name. Cecil Cratchley. Some had never taught in schools before, but it was all hands to the pump now – that's what Mr Flaker said, anyway. Needs must.

And the old people were the worst for caning. The young teachers before the war didn't do it so much, but Mr Flaker could barely get through a lesson without beating a boy. Mr Grace, who had been a valet at Buckingham Palace until he turned sixty-five, even kept a stick up his sleeve with a metal weight taped to the top of it. He called the stick Excalibur. Almost everyone had been on the receiving end of it at one time or another. Not that the boys complained much; most of them got a slap at home for the slightest thing. Only Alfie had never been struck by his parents – Georgie and Margie said they didn't believe in it – and when he mentioned this one day to Mr Grace, he went home with Excalibur's mark seared deeply into his left hand as punishment for his cheek.

Today, however, wasn't a Monday and it wasn't a

Thursday, so there would be no history and there would be no reading. It was a Tuesday, and so when Alfie was fully dressed, he reached into the back of his wardrobe and pulled out the wooden shoeshine box that he kept there. He placed it on the carpet, opening the lid carefully. The pungent smell of two boxes of polish seeped out, and he checked that everything he needed was inside: his brushes, his shine mitts, his jars of polish, his shoe-horn, his horsehair brush and his leather balm. He checked to see how full everything was, but he'd only re-stocked from his earnings the previous Friday so it should be another two weeks at least before he'd have to buy anything new. When he was satisfied that he had what he needed, he closed the box, went downstairs, made sure that there were no dirty marks on his face – for he had learned long ago that he did better business when his hair was neatly combed and his skin clean – put his coat and scarf on and went out into the cold October morning.

Alfie Summerfield was the man of the house now, after all. And he had a living to earn.

4

YOUR KING AND COUNTRY WANTS YOU

The shoeshine box was made of dark brown mahogany. It was twice as long as it was wide, with a gold-coloured clasp to unlock the lid from the base which, when opened, revealed three compartments within.

The first contained two horsehair brushes, one black, one brown, with corrugated grips on the handles; the second revealed a set of four grey shining cloths and a pair of sponge daubers; the third held two tins of polish which had been almost full when Alfie found the box. Carved into the side was the word *Holzknecht* and an emblem that displayed an eagle soaring above a mountain, wild-eyed and dangerous. Secured to the underside of the lid was a footrest that could be taken out and attached to the top of the sealed box through a pair of thin grooves etched into the side. This was where a customer laid his foot when he was having his shoes shined.

When Alfie first brought the box back to his own bedroom, he had stared at it for a long time, running his fingers across the elegant woodwork and taking careful sniffs of the polish, which sent an irritating tickle up his nose. He had seen boxes like this before, of course, although none as beautifully designed and well cared for as Mr Janáček's. A few days after signing up, his father had taken him to King's Cross – he'd said they were going there to look at the trains, but that wasn't the real reason – and Alfie had seen Leonard Hopkins from number two shining shoes in a corner by the ticket counter and charging a penny a shine. It seemed to take him a long time to finish each shoe, though, for every time a pretty girl walked by, Leonard's eyes followed her as if he had become hypnotized, and only when his customer tapped him on the head did he turn back again.

The last anyone had heard, Leonard was stationed just outside Bruges. He'd been in a field hospital for three months before being sent back on active duty. He wasn't even seventeen yet.

He'd mentioned Leonard's job to Mr Janáček one evening, and Kalena's father had laughed and said that the problem with the English was that they always wanted someone else to serve them. The rich had their valets and footmen, their housekeepers and maids; the poor couldn't afford such luxuries so it made them feel good to have someone shine their shoes for them instead. It gave them a sense of importance.

'But there are some things that we can all do for ourselves, Alfie,' Mr Janáček had declared, lifting a shoe in one hand and a brush in the other. 'And this, my young friend, is one of them.'

Carefully examining the shoeshine box, Alfie felt certain that it had been in Mr Janáček's family for a long time, a family heirloom, and that he had brought it with him to London when he left Prague, for the best reason in the world: for love. Maybe he'd even used it himself to earn money before he'd opened his sweet shop. Or maybe he'd simply held onto it to shine his shoes. It was true that Mr Janáček was always very well turned out; he was famous on Damley Road for his dapper appearance.

'It's his European blood,' Margie said to Mrs Milchin and Mrs Welton one afternoon when she was finishing some ironing for Mrs Gawdley-Smith, who lived in one of the posh houses just off Henley Square and whose washing Margie had started to take in for tuppence a load. ('Every basket I get through, Alfie, is another tea on the table for us.') 'On the continent, men take pride in their appearance.'

'Oh, if I was twenty years younger and Fred was looking the other way,' said Mrs Welton with a laugh, and Mrs Milchin shook her head and pulled a face like she'd just drunk a mouthful of sour milk.

'I don't like to see a man so tidy,' she said. 'If you ask me, that Mr Janáček is not to be trusted.' But then, Mrs Milchin had taken against him long ago on account of his accent. That was just who she was. She didn't like foreigners.

Alfie didn't like to think that he was stealing the shoeshine box; he preferred to think of it as borrowing. He knew that stealing was a bad thing – David Candlemas from number thirteen had nearly gone to jail for stealing coal from the shed at the back of the Scutworths' house, a scandal that had set Damley Road aflame for weeks – but he was sure that Mr Janáček would approve of what he was doing and he promised himself that he would return it when the war was over and Kalena and her father finally returned to number six.

If that day ever came.

Not long after this, Margie came home wearing a troubled expression on her face and told him that she had something important to say. They went into the parlour, where Alfie sat opposite her, his hands on his knees, leaning forward in expectation.

'Alfie,' she said, not looking directly at him but staring into the fireplace instead. She didn't say anything for a long time, but Alfie decided he wouldn't speak until she did. He was afraid of what she was going to tell him and could already feel the tears beginning to brew at the back of his eyes. 'I have a bit of news for you,' she said finally.

'Is it good news?' asked Alfie.

'Well, it's not bad news,' she replied. 'It's just news, that's all. Information.'

'Is it about Dad?'

She turned quickly and looked at him now, and their eyes met. It had been almost three years since Georgie had stepped into that same room in his soldier's uniform and Margie had run crying from the room and Granny Summerfield had declared that they were finished, they were all finished.

'It's not about your father,' said Margie, shaking her head. 'Alfie, we've had this conversation before. He's on a secret mission for the Government, I told you that. That's why he can't get in touch with us any more. It's why he doesn't write and why we can't write to him.'

Dad's dead, thought Alfie.

'I thought you understood all about that?' continued Margie, her voice rising a little as Alfie set his jaw and felt his teeth grinding against each other. *Dad's dead.* He closed his eyes, and in his head he heard the sound of a train pulling into a station, the noise of its engines drowning out everything that his mother was saying . . . *dead-Dad's-dead-Dad's-dead-Dad's-dead* . . . Her lips were still moving, she was still talking, he knew she was, but he couldn't hear her. He was blocking out every sound and could only hear those two words repeated over and over in his head.

'Alfie, stop it!' cried Margie, pulling his hands away from his ears, and he opened his eyes now and swallowed hard. 'What's the matter with you, anyway?'

'I was thinking about something, that's all.'

'What were you thinking about?'

'Dad.'

Margie sighed. 'Alfie, if you want to talk about your father, we can talk about your father. Is that what you want?'

'Tell me the truth about him.'

'I've told you the truth.'

'I'm not a baby,' insisted Alfie. 'Tell me the truth.'

Margie hesitated; for a moment it looked as if she really *was* going to tell him the truth, but the sound of Mr Asquith's hooves passing down Damley Road, his head turning automatically as he passed number twelve, pulled them both out of the moment and Alfie knew that there was no point in asking.

'Tell me your news, then,' he said at last.

Margie shook her head. 'Oh Alfie,' she said with a sigh. 'I don't know that I have the energy now.'

'Tell me,' he insisted.

'I've got a job,' she said, shrugging her shoulders. 'At the hospital. I'm to be a Queen's Nurse.'

'What's that?' asked Alfie, frowning.

'You read the paper. I know you do,' she said, not knowing that Alfie only looked at the newspaper every day to read the numbers.

14278.

'There's so many soldiers coming back from the Front with terrible injuries,' continued Margie. 'And they need more nurses to look after them. I have to do my bit, Alfie, you can see that, can't you? I've always wanted to find something I might be good at. Maybe this is it. I think about your dad and—' She stopped speaking for a moment and bit her lip, then shook her head, changing tack. 'I can be of use, Alfie. You understand that, don't you? The more people who are of use, the quicker the war will come to an end.'

'The war will *never* come to an end,' shouted Alfie, leaning forward in his seat now. 'It's going to go on *for ever.*'

'That's not true,' said Margie. 'It has to end one day. Wars always do. The new ones can't start if the old ones don't end,' she added, smiling a little, but Alfie wasn't in the mood for jokes. 'Anyway, I've been offered six weeks' training at the hospital and then a job after that – shift work unfortunately, so there'll be a few changes around here for a while. You're going to have to look after yourself a bit more. You can do that, can't you? Granny Summerfield is only across the road anyway if you want to go over there.'

Alfie thought about it. He didn't much like the idea of looking after himself. He wanted things to be back the way they used to be, when Georgie and Margie were looking after him, and Granny Summerfield was always stopping by for a bit of a gossip, and Old Bill Hemperton next door would *rat-a-tat-tat* on the door and give Alfie a ha'penny to go and fetch his paper for him, and Kalena Janáček was still his best friend and not a person of special interest and hadn't been taken away for internment.

'We need the money, Alfie, that's the truth of it,' said Margie when he didn't say anything.

'But you're already taking in washing,' said Alfie.

'Don't remind me. I'll have to do all that in the middle of the day, between shifts.'

'And when will you sleep?'

'Oh, I'll sleep when I'm—' She stopped herself suddenly, her cheeks flushing scarlet. 'I don't have any choice, Alfie. Times are tight, you know that.' She hesitated and raised her voice in exasperation. 'We don't have any money, Alfie! We're barely getting by as it is. Granny Summerfield has said we can go and live with her, but I won't do that. This is our home, and while I have breath in my body I won't take it away from you when you've already lost so many other things. Anyway, how am I supposed to keep you in sweets if I don't work?' She smiled, hoping that he'd smile back.

'I don't need sweets,' said Alfie. 'I can give them up. There aren't as many now anyway. Almost none of the shops stock them.'

'We need food,' she said then. 'Alfie, we're perilously close to penury. Perilously close.'

Alfie opened his eyes wide. He had no idea what *perilously close to penury* meant, but it didn't sound good.

'If I go out to work, and take in Mrs Gawdley-Smith's washing, and maybe take a few extra night shifts, then we can eat. If I don't, then we can't. It's as simple as that. Food doesn't grow on trees, you know.'

'It does actually,' said Alfie. 'Some of it. The rest grows in the ground.'

Margie smiled and even laughed a little, which made Alfie happy. It had been a long time since he'd made his mother laugh. 'Well, that's true,' she said. 'But you know what I mean.'

In the end, they'd had a long talk about the hospital and the hours she would have to work, and Alfie promised that he wouldn't get into any trouble and that he'd go to school every day, which Margie said was a sign that he was growing up.

'You'll be a fine man one day, Alfie Summerfield,' she told him, kissing him on the top of his forehead. 'Just like your father. He'd be proud of you if he was here with us now.'

But he wasn't with them, of course. He didn't write, he didn't send telegrams; he didn't come home on leave like Jack Tamorin from number twenty or Arthur Morris from number eighteen. Margie insisted that his dad's secret mission would bring the war to an end more quickly, but Alfie didn't believe a word of it.

He knew that his father was dead.

Alfie stole Mr Janáček's shoeshine box for one reason only: so that he could go out to work like Leonard Hopkins had and help his mother out. She was doing her bit; it was time he did his bit too.

The next morning was a Wednesday so there was no need to go to school. (It wasn't reading or history that day, after all.) Alfie waited until Margie left for her first week's training at the hospital and then took the box out of the wardrobe, opened it to make sure that everything was still in place, had a wash, got dressed, ate some breakfast, and left the house.

Damley Road was only a short walk from King's Cross, and Alfie made his way along the familiar streets, switching the box from his right hand to his left whenever it grew too heavy. He felt like a man of the world, a working man just like his dad had once been, getting up early to ride the milk float. When he passed other working men on the street, he felt an urge to tip his cap to them, but didn't do so in case it made him look stupid.

As he stepped inside the station, he felt a great wave of emotion overtake him. The last time he'd been here – the *only* time he'd been here – was when Georgie had taken him a few days after he'd signed up. The station had been very busy then. Newspaper boys were everywhere – it was said that during July 1914, circulation increased six-fold as everyone wanted to find out what might happen to them next – and there were hundreds of people boarding and leaving the trains. The noise of the steam engines was deafening and the station itself was filled with a smog as bad as any of the London pea-soupers. Georgie wasn't wearing his soldier's uniform that day. It was hanging in his wardrobe at home. He hadn't put it on again since he'd stepped into the front parlour and surprised them all.

'Do you know,' said Georgie, standing in the concourse and looking around at the platforms, staring at the height of the station ceiling and listening to the sound of the conductors' whistles, 'I used to think I might like to be a train driver. I tried for a job on the London-to-Edinburgh line but I didn't get it.'

'Why not?' asked Alfie, looking up at his dad.

'They said I wasn't a good fit,' he replied with a shrug. 'Whatever that meant. They're a posh old lot, them train drivers. They think they're better than everyone else on account of how they get to wear a uniform all the time. But they're not.'

'You're going to wear a uniform now too,' said Alfie, and Georgie laughed a little and tousled the boy's hair even though Alfie hadn't meant it as a joke.

'Yes, I expect I am,' he said. 'Hold on now – since we're here there's a bit of business I need to take care of.'

They walked over towards the ticket counter, where lots of people were queuing up for tickets, but at the end of the row were three desks lined up on the platform without railings in front of them, each one manned by an officer, leaning over ledgers and making notes alongside some of the entries.

'Afternoon,' said Georgie, lighting up a cigarette and taking a drag from it as he approached the man at the centre table, who was about ten years older than him and had dark black hair, parted neatly at the side and with so much hair cream in it that his comb had left teeth marks like a freshly ploughed field. Alfie heard a wolf whistle and turned round to see Leonard Hopkins, kneeling by his shoeshine box, leering at a girl who turned in surprise and smiled, before being dragged away by her mother.

'Can I help you?' said the man behind the desk.

'The name's Georgie Summerfield,' said Georgie. 'I was told to come along to organize my transport.'

'You're a new recruit, are you?'

'That's right.'

The man behind the desk nodded but wore a very serious expression on his face. He glanced at the men on either side of him, who exchanged an amused look before shaking their heads and getting back to their ledgers.

'All right then, son,' said the man in the middle. 'You're new at all this, so I'll assume that you don't understand the way we do things around here. First things first: take the cigarette out of your mouth and put it out.'

Georgie stared at the man and Alfie stared at Georgie. Something changed on his dad's face – a sudden realization that life was different now to what it had been a few days before. He did what he was told, tossing the cigarette onto the ground and crushing it beneath the heel of his boot. Alfie noticed a slight tremor in his hands as he did so.

'Now stand up straight and look ahead, there's a good fellow. You're not an animal in the jungle. Posture. At all times, posture.'

Georgie adjusted his stance, standing to his full height, shoulders back, eyes looking straight ahead. Beside him, Alfie did the same thing. His head came up to his dad's waist.

'That's better. Now let's try this again, shall we? I think what you meant to say was, Good afternoon, sir.'

'Yes, sir,' said Georgie.

'Your name again?'

'Georgie Summerfield.'

The sergeant raised an eyebrow and put his pen back on the table, staring at Alfie's dad with an irritated expression on his face.

'Georgie Summerfield, sir,' whispered Alfie.

'Georgie Summerfield, sir,' repeated Georgie in a quiet, resigned voice.

The sergeant nodded and leafed through a book, running his finger along a list of names. 'Damley Road?' he asked, looking up.

'That's right, sir.'

'You're in luck, Summerfield. You've got a few days yet. Wednesday morning. Eight a.m. transport from Liverpool Street. Aldershot Barracks. Basic training for eight weeks. Bring this with you on the morning' – he handed a ticket across – 'and you'll see our lot soon enough on platform four. 14278 – that's your number. Don't be late, there's a good chap. We call that desertion.'

'Right you are, sir.'

The sergeant looked at Alfie. 'And who's this blighter, then?' he asked.

'That's my boy, sir. Alfie.'

'Proud of your old man, are you, Alfie?' asked the sergeant, but Alfie didn't say anything. 'Well, you will be,' he went on, dismissing them both now. 'One day.'

'I thought we came to look at the trains,' said Alfie when they were walking home.

'We did,' said Georgie.

'No we didn't,' said Alfie, pulling his hand free of his dad's as they walked along.

Now Alfie was back in King's Cross for the first time since that day. He looked around, remembering where the sergeant had sat, but there were no desks there now, although the location of the ticket counters hadn't changed. There were a lot of soldiers to be seen making their way across the concourse. Some were waiting in small groups beside the teashop, their rucksacks on the ground beside them. Others were climbing down off trains and looking around for people they recognized. The rhythmic noise of the engines was as bad as ever – *dead-Dad's-dead-Dad's-dead-Dad's-dead* – and Alfie wondered how the people who worked here could bear it.

He noticed one young Tommy standing in the centre of a platform with a bag on his back and a deep red scar running down the side of his face. He was about twenty years old, Alfie thought, and had an expression on his face that was difficult to define; it was as if he'd been visited by a ghost but didn't know how to tell anyone in case they locked him up and threw away the key. A moment later, two older people, a man and a woman – his parents, Alfie was certain of it – ran towards him, and when he saw them his rucksack fell off his back and his face collapsed. He looked as if he was about to fall over, but before he could, his mother and father were on either side of him, holding him up, and he was crying on their shoulders, great heavy sobs, as they wrapped him up between their bodies, protecting him from the world, rubbing his hair and whispering in his ears. When they started to walk away, the boy remained between them, and they stood as close as they could without all falling down in a muddle. The father's arm was wrapped around his son's shoulders; the mother's clasped tight around the boy's waist. Alfie watched them for a long time until he decided he shouldn't stare like this, and then he turned away.

He looked around and was pleased to see that there were no other shoeshine boys in King's Cross. Leonard Hopkins was long gone, and no one, it seemed, had come to take his place. He chose a point by a pillar that was equidistant from the ticket counter on his left and the platforms on his right and the teashop in the corner, and sat down on the ground, opening Mr Janáček's box, taking out his brushes, cloths, daubers and polishes, and closed the lid. He took his cap off his head and placed it upside down on the ground next to him before throwing the loose change from his pocket – three ha'pennies – into it to make it look like he'd already started. And then he looked up and shouted at the top of his voice:

'Shoeshine! Get your shoes shined here!'

Later that day, when he got home, he found Margie having a nap in the front parlour; she looked exhausted. He ran upstairs to his room and put the box at the back of his wardrobe before coming back down to the kitchen and washing his hands with carbolic soap. When he was finished, he gave them a sniff but they still smelled of polish so he did it all over again. It wasn't much better, but there was nothing he could do about it; they were as clean as he could get them for now. His back hurt a little from leaning over all day and the muscles in his arms were sore. There might have been a war going on, but there was still a surprising number of people who wanted their shoes to look good.

He looked around and felt his heart sink with what he saw. All the chairs were covered with Mrs Gawdley-Smith's pillow cases, and the line outside in the yard held her bed sheets and some funny-looking undergarments. Margie would never smell the polish on his hands, after all. The place smelled too much like a laundry.

He found his mother's purse in the handbag that was sitting in the corner and took it out, opening the clasp and looking inside. There wasn't much money there. Reaching into his pocket, he took out all his earnings from the day and dropped most of it inside – enough money that she'd be pleased to find it there but not so much that she'd question where it had appeared from – before taking the rest back up to his bedroom, where he hid it in a box at the back of his sock drawer for a rainy day. Then he collapsed on his bed and closed his eyes.

It was still early evening, the sun was shining outside, but Alfie was asleep on top of his bed while Margie was snoring in the broken armchair in front of the fireplace.

It had never been like this before the war began.

5

WHEN THIS LOUSY WAR IS OVER

Alfie started work at eight o'clock in the morning, one of the busiest times of the day at King's Cross. He took up his usual position with a view of the platforms, the ticket counter and the teashop, pulled over a seat for his customers, threw his upturned cap on the ground and looked around for his first shine of the day. While he waited, he took *Robinson Crusoe* from his pocket and picked up where he'd left off the night before. The edges had grown a little scruffy, the paper was a little torn, but the words were all intact.

'Hello, Alfie!'

He looked up to see Mr Podgett, a local bank manager who got his shoes shined every week, standing before him.

'Hello, Mr Podgett,' replied Alfie.

'The usual please,' he said, sitting down and unfolding his newspaper as he placed one foot on the footrest and let out a great sigh of comfort.

Alfie took a look at his dark brown shoes; they were a little dusty at the tips and had suffered a number of scuffs since the previous week. 'Cold morning, isn't it? Well, it is almost November, I suppose. Can't expect a heat wave.'

Alfie took out his dusting cloths and wiped Mr Podgett's left shoe clean before dipping a buffing cloth in the tin of polish and spreading an even coat across the surface of the shoe. Then he picked up the brown horsehair brush and began to run it briskly over the clean area. He quite liked the smell of polish; it reminded him of when he used to run into number six to play with Kalena. Her house always smelled like this.

'Better news today,' said Mr Podgett as he scanned the headlines. 'Looks like things are going our way for a change. Maybe this blasted war will come to an end soon after all. I said to Mrs Podgett this morning, *Mrs Podgett,* I said, *I think it's only going to be a few more months before the end is upon us.* Of course, she claims that I say that all the time and it never comes true, and perhaps she's right, but this time I really believe it.'

Alfie said nothing. He knew from experience that Mr Podgett preferred to talk and talk without being interrupted. It was better not to speak until he was asked a direct question that required an answer.

'Our son, Billy, is still over there of course,' he

added after a moment. 'I've told you about Billy, haven't I? He's somewhere in Belgium with his battalion. Can't say where, of course. All very top secret, hush hush and on the QT. He has more than three hundred men under his command, if you can believe it. Of course, he was always very responsible and conscientious, even as a boy. Never gave us a moment's trouble. You're the same, I'd imagine, aren't you, Alfie? A credit to your family.'

'Mum says I'm a proper handful,' said Alfie.

'Well, I'm sure you don't mean to be. But Billy was always well-behaved so it's no surprise that he's gone on to earn such responsibility. All right, there was that incident when we went to Cornwall to visit his Aunt Harriet and he got into a terrible fight with the Cattermole boy, but that was something and nothing, I always said, and should never have been allowed to develop into such a fuss. The boy was all right in the end, after all? It wasn't as if he was in hospital for more than a couple of days. And as for that girl, the one who said she'd witnessed it all, well, she was a flighty piece, everyone knew that. There was talk about her – I won't say what kind of talk, Alfie, on account of your young ears, but let's be honest, there's no smoke without fire, is there, and it's hard not to imagine that she was playing one of them off against the other. Ever been to Cornwall, Alfie?'

'No, sir,' said Alfie.

'Beautiful part of the world. Where do you go on your holidays, then? The Lake District? Wales? Somewhere up north?'

Alfie tried not to laugh. Sometimes adults asked the stupidest questions. He'd never been on a holiday in his life. He wasn't even entirely sure what you did on one. Was it the same things you did on any other day, only in a different location? If his family went on holiday, would he be shining shoes on Blackpool Pier? Would Granny Summerfield be looking for a bit of a gossip at Stonehenge? Would Margie be struggling to make ends meet on the Isle of Wight?

'Of course, things worked out quite well for the Cattermole boy in the end,' continued Mr Podgett, not waiting for an answer. 'Harriet told me that he wasn't able to go to the war on account of how his leg never healed correctly afterwards, but I can't imagine that had anything to do with Billy. Might have even done it deliberately to avoid being conscripted. You hear stories like that all the time, don't you? Disgraceful business. I'd have more respect for a conchie than I would for someone like that. No, if you ask me, Billy did the boy a favour, and now look at him! Somewhere in the middle of Europe, leading five hundred men in and out of danger zones, putting the welfare of his country before his own safety. He wrote to his mother recently and said that he hoped the war would never end, that's how much he enjoys the fighting, but I can't imagine he meant it. Everyone wants the war to end. Mrs Podgett, she burst into tears when she read that letter; she said that it was all our fault that he turned out like he did, but I said, *Alice, what are you talking about? Our son has a thousand men under his command and he's proved his worth time and again, leading all those brave men into battle, writing to the parents of every boy who's been killed. Why, he can't even go over the top himself any more on account of how much writing he has to do.* No, he's a fine boy, Alfie, I'm proud of him, but it says here' – and with that he tapped on the newspaper once again – 'it says here that things are looking up and maybe there's an end in sight. That'd be good, wouldn't it? You'd like to see an end to the war, I expect?'

Alfie nodded. He'd finished with the left shoe by now and had started on the right. This was a direct question. It required an answer.

'I would, sir, yes,' he said.

'Well, of course you would. Everyone would. Heavens above, boy, that's a fine shine there on that shoe. You should do this for a living.'

'I already do,' muttered Alfie quietly.

'I tell all my colleagues at the bank about you. I expect you've seen a few of them here? You should have me on commission, you really should. Or at least give me a free shine every now and then.' He laughed when he said this but Alfie didn't think he was joking. He put his head down and got on with his polishing.

'All done?' asked Mr Podgett finally when Alfie gave them a last dusting and sat up to admire his work.

'Yes, sir,' said Alfie.

'Very good.' He stood up and threw a penny in Alfie's cap, hesitating for a moment as he looked down at the boy. 'I did my best for him, of course,' he said finally, his voice quieter than usual. 'Maybe if I could go back . . . but you can't, can you?' He shook his head, and now he was almost whispering. 'Even if you wanted to.' Alfie stared at him, uncertain what he was expected to say, and Mr Podgett looked back with a sorrowful expression on his face and simply shook his head. 'You remind me a little of him, you know,' he said. 'When he was a boy. He had an open face, like yours. There was kindness there once. Anyway . . .' He sighed and shook his head, looking up at the station clock. 'I better be getting on. Same time next week, Alfie? You'll be here?'

'Yes, sir,' said Alfie.

'All right, then,' said Mr Podgett, raising a hand in the air in salute as he walked away. 'Until then, *auf Wiedersehen*, Alfie, as our Hun friends say.'

Which wasn't very wise of him, for three

different heads turned as he departed and a man walked over to a constable and whispered something in his ear; a moment later, the policeman was following Mr Podgett out of the station and on to the busy streets beyond.

By eleven o'clock, Alfie had shined three sets of shoes and spent a ha'penny on a sausage roll from the teashop, which left him tuppence ha'penny up on the day so far. He'd seen a man be refused passage on the London-to-Cambridge train on account of drunkenness, and a small girl, only a year or so younger than him, had stuck her tongue out at him as she walked past, hand in hand with an elderly lady.

A man with a bright red moustache had put up a series of recruitment posters around the station: one showed a night-time image of London, with Big Ben and St Paul's Cathedral to the foreground. IT IS FAR BETTER TO FACE THE BULLETS THAN TO BE KILLED AT HOME BY A BOMB, it said. Another showed a smiling Tommy, clean and cheerful, with a rifle on his back. FOLLOW ME! it said. YOUR COUNTRY NEEDS YOU. Alfie didn't imagine that many of the soldiers looked that happy in real life.

Just after noon, a young man passed by his shoeshine stand, glanced at him, walked on and then stopped for a moment, looking up at the enormous clock on the wall. He checked his ticket before looking back at Alfie and down at his own shoes. He was about twenty-five years old and carried a cane in his left hand. As he made his way back, his bad leg dragged a little and Alfie tried not to stare. He wore a dark suit, a crisp white shirt and a black tie, and he didn't seem at all comfortable in any of them.

'I think I could do with a polish,' said the young man, his voice betraying a mixture of refinement and anxiety. A moment later, he laughed a little, and Alfie didn't know why; it was as if he was sharing a joke with himself. He sat down, placed his left shoe on the footrest, and Alfie got to work.

'Busy this morning?' asked the man.

'Not very,' said Alfie, looking up. 'Tuesday's always a bit quiet. I don't know why. Monday's the busiest day because everyone wants clean shoes for the start of the week but I don't work on a Monday.'

'Any special reason?'

'We do history in school on Monday. I don't like to miss it.'

The young man laughed. 'Very sensible,' he said. 'I was never any good at history. I could never get my head round the kings and queens, the battles and the wars. All those stories about the dukes in the Tower—'

'The princes,' said Alfie.

'Who was it who put them there, Richard the Second?'

'Richard the Third,' said Alfie.

'Names and numbers, that's what it felt like to me, names and numbers. Good for you that you like it. My name's Wilf, by the way,' he said.

'Alfie,' said Alfie, thinking how nothing ever changed; more than four hundred years later, and everything was names and numbers once again.

'Nice to meet you, Alfie. Give them a good buff, will you, there's a good chap. I can't show up with dirty shoes. I took them out of the wardrobe this morning and couldn't believe the condition they were in, even though I haven't worn them in ages.'

Alfie looked up as his hands ran a sponge dauber along the welt of the shoe. It crossed his mind that since he'd started working at King's Cross he'd learned instinctively when someone wanted to talk and when someone wanted to be left in peace. Men like Mr Podgett enjoyed the sound of their own voices. Others, like Wilf, seemed as if they wanted a bit of a conversation. And as far as Alfie was concerned, that was all part of the job.

'Going somewhere nice, sir?' he asked.

'Cheltenham,' said Wilf. 'Nice place; not a nice reason.'

Alfie looked up and understood immediately why the young man was wearing black.

'My brother's funeral,' explained Wilf. 'My

younger brother, that is. Alistair. They brought his body back this weekend.'

'I'm sorry,' said Alfie.

'Yes,' replied Wilf, the word catching in his throat a little. 'Yes, so am I. Only eighteen years old, you see. The youngest of us all. And the brightest. I only saw him about a month ago. He was shipping out of Aldershot on his way to Calais. I went down to Southampton to wish him luck.'

Alfie stopped buffing when he heard that word – *Aldershot.* That was where Georgie had been sent for training. He'd stayed there for a couple of months, learning to fight, learning to kill, before being sent to France, where he'd written to them every week for almost two years before the letters suddenly stopped and Margie said that he couldn't write any more, on account of the fact that he was on a secret mission for the Government.

Which, as far as Alfie was concerned, was an adult way of saying that your father is dead but we don't want to tell you the truth.

'Alistair got himself killed only a couple of weeks after he arrived, poor chap,' continued Wilf. 'I don't know if it was a blessing for him or a tragedy. He didn't have to spend years in the trenches like some of the other poor souls over there. He's out of it now, isn't he?'

'What happened to him?' asked Alfie, looking up, knowing he shouldn't ask questions like this, but the words were out of his mouth before he could pull them back.

'Some fool of a sergeant sent him over the top in the middle of the night as a stretcher bearer,' said Wilf. 'It's a suicide mission, isn't it? Collecting the dead. No one can survive it. There should be an hour's armistice when both sides can go over and collect their fallen soldiers. I suggested it once, at GHQ, and the way the generals looked at me you would have sworn I was waving the white flag of surrender. All I wanted was a bit of civilized behaviour in an uncivilized world. Still, Alistair wouldn't have felt a thing, which is something, I suppose. But by God, it took them long enough to ship the body home. The funeral's later today. The War Office gave me the day off. So it's over to Cheltenham and back for me, and no time to spend with my family. I have to be at my desk again first thing tomorrow morning or there'll be hell to pay.'

Alfie glanced over at Wilf's cane, which was propped up against the chair next to him. His eyes lingered there for a moment before he realized that Wilf was watching him.

'Wondering about this, are you?' he asked. 'It's kept me out of it for the last two years. Took a sniper bullet through my femur just outside Mons. Lay in a field hospital for a week or two while they tried to save the leg. Nothing doing, of course. Would have saved a lot of time and energy if they'd just cut the blighter off the day I arrived instead of waiting for two whole months.'

Alfie stopped what he was doing, his hands hovering in the air over Wilf's left shoe.

'Oh yes, that's a false leg, I'm afraid,' he said. 'Don't be frightened, boy. There's nothing to fear.'

Alfie shook his head and went back to his shoe shining. 'I'm not frightened,' he said quietly.

'We live in strange times when a man needs to shine a shoe for his false leg, don't we?' said Wilf with a half-smile. 'Still, one must keep up appearances. That's what they tell us, anyway. A strange thing: I'm damned glad to be out of it and yet I feel like I'm shirking my duty, stuck over here. Ended up with a desk job at the War Office, you see. They took my uniform away from me, told me to wear a suit. They've no idea what it's like for men my age out of uniform. The looks we get. A woman came up to me in the middle of Piccadilly Circus, perhaps she didn't notice my cane. Opened her handbag, and in front of everyone she . . . she . . .' He shook his head, his lip curling in a mixture of anger and pain. 'Why do they do that?' he muttered. 'They don't understand, any of them.'

Alfie felt uncomfortable being confronted by so much pain and anger. He noticed a split in the brown pupil of the man's right eye: a birthmark of some sort.

'Do you have any older brothers over there?'

asked Wilf after a moment, and Alfie shook his head. 'Your dad, then? Sorry, I shouldn't ask. It's none of my business, really.'

'How do they look?' asked Alfie, nodding at the young man's shoes; he was finished at last. He was glad to be finished.

'Spot on. Couldn't have done better myself.' He took a penny from his pocket and threw it in the centre of Alfie's cap. It made a ringing sound as it bounced off the coins from earlier. 'Thank you,' he said, standing up now and reaching for his cane. He opened his mouth to say something else, but seemed to think better of it and simply walked away without another word, heading towards platform six, disappearing into the heart of the crowd as Alfie watched him for a few moments and then reorganized all his shining equipment on the ground beside him, waiting for his next customer.

Alfie didn't eat much for lunch. All that bending over the shoeshine box seemed to kill his appetite a little. The smell of the polish and the fact that the steam from the engines was catching in his throat didn't help either. But he knew that he wouldn't be able to work as hard in the afternoon if he didn't have something, so he managed a small steak-and-kidney pie from the food stall. The pastry was heavy and dry and there was more gravy than meat inside – he was sure there had only been one bite of steak and two gristly pieces of kidney – but it filled him up for now.

Business was slow in the afternoon and the day had grown colder. A strong breeze was pouring through from the exit on Euston Road and rattling around the platform, forcing the commuters to wrap their coats tighter around themselves. Between two and four o'clock there were never many customers, which meant that Alfie could spend more time on the Island of Despair with *Robinson Crusoe*, but he knew that the early evening crowds would start pouring through soon, and when they did he might get a customer or two.

A little after half past three, a thin middle-aged man wearing a brown military uniform that looked as if it had been freshly pressed about ten minutes earlier sat down without a word and placed his right foot on the footrest. Alfie said nothing and simply got to work as the man pulled a document folder from his briefcase and gave his full attention to the thick file in his hands, shaking his head every so often and muttering rude words under his breath. When he said one that was *very* rude, Alfie sniggered a little and dropped his polish jar. Immediately the man put his folder down and stared at the boy.

'What was that?' he said after a moment.

'Sorry, sir,' said Alfie.

The man shook his head. 'No, *I'm* sorry,' he said. 'Was I talking to myself again?'

Alfie nodded and the man laughed. 'It's a habit of mine,' he said. 'My wife's always telling me off about it.' He put the folder aside for a moment and watched as Alfie picked up a cloth and ran it across his left heel. 'You're very good at that,' he said finally. 'Been at it a while, have you?'

'More than a year, sir,' said Alfie.

'Good Lord. How old are you, boy?'

'Nine, sir.'

'Nine years old and already earning a living. It's like being back in Dickens's time. Ever read Dickens?'

'No, sir.'

'Ever read anything?'

'Yes, sir.'

'What?'

'*Robinson Crusoe.*'

'I haven't read that since I was a boy. Read *Oliver Twist.* Or *Nicholas Nickleby.* I promise you'll enjoy them. I'm reading this new chap, Lawrence, but I don't think he'd be right for you just yet. Shouldn't you be in school anyway?'

Alfie looked up but said nothing and the man simply shrugged his shoulders and looked away. 'None of my business, I suppose,' he said. 'I have enough to concern myself with as it is without worrying about the well-being of every waif and stray I run into.'

Some of the polish was clogging up the bristles on Alfie's brush, and he shook it out, rubbing it against the floor to remove the grit, leaving a grimy residue on the tiles beside him. The man didn't say anything else as Alfie worked but returned to his folders instead, turning the pages quickly, making notes on some of them with an expensive-looking pen, drawing great lines through others. The breeze from the street outside picked up, sending a rush of air through the station, and just as the man turned a page, he lost hold of his folder, and all his documents were swept out of his hands, scattering loose pages all around the concourse.

'Oh!' he cried, jumping up, almost kicking Alfie as his right foot lifted off the shoeshine box. 'My papers! I can't lose them. Help me, there's a good chap. Grab as many as you can before they float away.'

Alfie ran around the station, gathering great handfuls as he went; they were everywhere – over by the teashop, close to the ticket counter, near the tobacconist's, next to the newspaper stall. But he grabbed and he grabbed, and before he knew it he had more than forty pages in his hands, and as he looked around, trying to see whether there were any more in sight, his eyes fell on the top page that he was holding.

It was an official-looking document, fancy writing and expensive paper, with the words EAST

SUFFOLK & IPSWICH HOSPITAL inscribed across the top and Latin writing underneath, even though no one could speak Latin any more. Typed underneath were the words:

Returnees – One Page Review

And beneath that, in smaller type, the sentence:

Refer to File 3(b) for full patient assessments.

There were two columns, left and right, listing names and serial numbers, with another number listed after that which Alfie assumed had something to do with File 3(b). He didn't mean to read the list of names along the left-hand column – he wasn't really interested – but the problem was that it was a page filled with words, and for as long as Alfie could remember, whenever he saw pages filled with words he wanted to read them. His eyes glanced across the records and quickly settled on one single entry.

He blinked, uncertain whether he could believe the evidence of his own eyes, almost dropping all the papers that he had collected. And just at that moment, the man from the shoeshine stand stepped forward and plucked all the documents out of his hand.

'That's all of them, I think,' he said, looking

around the station as he piled the pages back inside his folder. 'Thanks for your help, boy. How much do I owe you?'

Alfie said nothing; simply stared up at the man, open-mouthed. He couldn't find any words to answer. There were too many things running through his brain.

'What's the matter with you?' the man asked. 'Cat got your tongue?'

And still Alfie remained silent. The man raised an eyebrow and shook his head, as if to suggest that he didn't have time for any more of this nonsense before saying, 'We'll call it a penny, shall we?' He tossed a coin into Alfie's hat, picked up his briefcase and turned away before stopping and looking back once again.

'Are you quite all right, boy?' he asked, his tone a little more sympathetic now. 'It's just that I'm a doctor, you see. And you look as if you've had a funny turn. If there's anything wrong, you can tell me. I might be able to help.'

Alfie shook his head. 'I'm fine,' he said, the words coming out in a croak, the way they did whenever Margie woke him too early in the morning.

'All right, then,' said the doctor, shrugging his shoulders and turning away. 'Thanks for the shine.'

Slowly Alfie made his way back over to his

shoeshine box and sat down on the customers' seat. He picked up all his cloths and brushes and polishes and put them away, removed the footrest from the top and replaced it under the lid before snapping the entire thing shut with the gold catch. Then, standing up, he made his way out of King's Cross and began to walk home.

And all the way there he thought of the single line that had jumped out at him from the East Suffolk & Ipswich Hospital document.

A simple phrase written halfway down the page, on the left-hand side.

Summerfield, George, it had said.

DOB: 3/5/1887.

Serial no.: 14278.

6

FOR ME AND MY GIRL

On the way back from the station, Alfie remembered the day his father left; how he wouldn't allow anyone to come to Liverpool Street to see him off.

'I know what it'll be like down there,' he said, shaking his head. 'All those wives and mothers crying into their hankies, making a spectacle of themselves. Let's just say our goodbyes here and be done with it. It's not like I'll be gone long anyway. It'll all be over by Christmas.'

He was leaving for Aldershot Barracks to begin basic training, and Alfie could tell that he was both excited and nervous to be going. After he signed up, Margie refused to speak to him for two days and only came around when it was clear that his mind was made up and there was nothing she could do about it. Even Granny Summerfield stopped declaring that they were finished, they were all finished, and started telling everyone on Damley Road how proud she was of her son, for he was one of the first to enlist, to answer the call of king and country, and he would surely be kept safe on account of his bravery.

As he left number twelve, Margie threw her arms around his neck and whispered into his ear something that made him bite his lip and hug her even closer. The neighbours came out of their houses to see him off, and Joe Patience pressed a packet of Golden Virginia tobacco into Georgie's hand and wished him luck.

'Don't do anything I wouldn't do,' he said, which made Alfie's dad laugh and shake his head.

'You won't be far behind him, I suppose,' said Granny Summerfield, looking back and forth between her son in his uniform and Joe in a pair of trousers and a working man's shirt. 'You and Georgie were always thick as thieves. I'm surprised you didn't sign up together.' There was a note of hostility in her voice and Joe couldn't meet her eye.

'There are plenty of ways to help the war effort,' he said. 'I'm not sure that killing people is the most productive.'

'Well, you might not have any choice,' she replied. 'It's all volunteers now, but if things don't go our way, then—'

'There's always a choice, Mrs Summerfield,' insisted Joe, a little more steel entering his voice now. 'I make up my own mind about things, you know that.'

Granny Summerfield's face grew red with anger, but Georgie said that this wasn't a morning for politics, that he just wanted to shake hands with his friends and hug his family, and reluctantly she stopped talking. But it was obvious that she had a lot more to say.

The last person Georgie said goodbye to was Alfie, who was standing in the street with his back pressed up against the front parlour window.

'You're the man of the house now,' he said, looking him directly in the eye, and Alfie felt his stomach sink at the idea of so much responsibility. 'You'll watch out for your mother while I'm away, won't you? And your granny?'

'Yes,' said Alfie. 'But you'll come home again, won't you?'

'Before you've even noticed that I've gone.'

And with that, he strolled down the street with his kitbag on his back as if he was simply going to the dairy for a day's work, before stopping and turning, lifting a hand in the air to wave goodbye, and then disappearing round the corner. But that was nearly four years ago now, and Alfie hadn't laid eyes on his father since then.

There were letters, of course. The first came from Aldershot: he told his family that the train journey had been great fun and that everyone was excited about what was ahead of them. Most of the new recruits were from London, but there were a couple of boys from Norwich and Ipswich, and even a Plymouth lad who'd only moved to Clapham six months earlier to take up a job on the buses. A fellow called Sergeant Clayton was in charge and he made them line up in the courtyard and tell him their names. He played the tartar something awful, Georgie said, shouting at anyone who didn't say *Yes, sir, No, sir, Three bags full, sir.* He had two corporals with him, Wells and Moody, standing on either side, saying very little.

The barracks have two rows of ten beds each [Georgie told them]. *I'm near the door with a boy called Mitchell on one side of me – Arsenal supporter, but I won't hold that against him – and another called Jonesy on the other. And you won't believe this, Alfie, but Jonesy only has a copy of that book that Mr Janáček gave you for your birthday. Robinson Crusoe! I nearly laughed when I saw it, I swear I did.*

Margie kept Georgie's letters safe and didn't like Alfie to handle them in case they got dirty. When Granny Summerfield was holding one up to her eyes so she could see it better, he could see his mum watching nervously, wishing that she'd just let her read it aloud to her like she'd offered to do at the start.

'He makes it sound like it's just a big game,' said Granny Summerfield when she had finished one of the early letters, and Margie took it back quickly and placed it between the pages of her Bible. 'I thought I brought him up to be smarter than that.'

'If he was smart, then he wouldn't have signed up in the first place,' said Margie.

Of course, things were different now that Alfie was nine. No one was volunteering any more. There was conscription. You reached the age of eighteen and that was it. You had to go to the war. Alfie spent a lot of time thinking that if they didn't sort things out in the next nine years, then he'd be going to the war too, an idea that frightened him. It didn't matter any more if you were married so there was no point in taking your sweetheart to the church to get out of serving. Even if you did, you'd be going off to France on your honeymoon alone.

Unless you were Joe Patience, that is, who had only just come back to number sixteen after two years away, although he hadn't been serving in France or fighting in Belgium. Instead, he'd been locked up in Wormwood Scrubs because he refused to become a soldier. They only let him out again because he'd suffered so many beatings inside; the last one had come so close to killing him that there'd been the threat of a prison scandal. Now Joe was back living two doors up, but almost never left his house and certainly never sat outside playing his clarinet like he did before the war began. Granny Summerfield called him a scoundrel and a coward, Mrs Milchin said that he should be strung up on the nearest lamp post. Even Helena Morris, who used to be sweet on him, said that he shouldn't be allowed to live near decent, respectable people.

Only Margie and Old Bill Hemperton still had anything to do with him. Margie insisted that he was Georgie's oldest friend and that whatever the rights and wrongs of his situation, he'd suffered enough for his beliefs. Old Bill simply said that he was his own man too and wouldn't be told who he could and couldn't speak to, not while there was still breath in his body. Neither of which was a good enough excuse to satisfy Granny Summerfield, who couldn't hear the man's name spoken aloud without flying into a rage.

Three months after he turned the corner of Damley Road, Georgie was no longer in England. Along with the other new soldiers, he took a train to Southampton and from there a boat to Calais, and after that his letters started to arrive less frequently, and when they did they sometimes had great black marks through the lines so Alfie and his mum couldn't read every word.

'That's the bosses,' explained Margie. 'They read everyone's letters and if there's anything in there that they don't want us to know about, they cross it out. They don't want us to know the truth. They're afraid of it.'

The tone of Georgie's letters changed over time. When he was in training at Aldershot he used to tell stories about the pranks the men played on each other at the barracks and the trouble they were always getting into with Sergeant Clayton. It sounded more like a holiday camp than anything else. But when he got to France, everything changed. He stopped talking about the soldiers serving alongside him and just talked about himself; about how he was feeling.

It's horrible here [he wrote]. *We spend our days digging trenches seven feet deep in the mud, then before they collapse we have to build wooden fortifications at the side. They say the Germans have steel walls on theirs. Whenever it rains, the sides of our trenches cave in and we have to use whatever we can find to scoop the water out. Sometimes I use my helmet but I'm not supposed to, as that's the quickest way to get a bullet through the head. There's rats everywhere. And worse. I could live with the rats. I don't know what half these creatures are. Why did I come here, I don't know. God, what a mistake.*

Margie didn't let Alfie read this letter. But he knew it had come because he'd seen it on the mat, the War Office seal displayed prominently on the envelope. 'It's private,' Margie told him after she read it in the broken armchair in front of the fireplace. 'Just between your father and me. But he says he loves you and he thinks about you all the time.'

'Read it out,' said Alfie.

'No.'

'Read it out!'

'I said no!' cried Margie, leaping up so quickly that Alfie jumped back in surprise. At which point she simply stared at him, looked as if she might burst into tears, and ran from the room.

She didn't put this letter between the pages of the Bible. Instead she hid it underneath her mattress, but Alfie knew all Margie's hiding places and waited until she was gone to work to read it. He read it five times, and each time it made him sadder and sadder.

After this, Margie didn't let him read any of the letters that came, but she put them in the same place so he always knew where to find them and where to hide them again whenever she called up the stairs to him.

God, Margie, what am I doing here? It's awful. And I've done terrible things. Can't live with myself sometimes. I think of you and

'Alfie, I'm home! Are you upstairs? Come down and tell me how your day was!'

They say we're getting closer to the Belgian lines but

it's hard to believe we're getting closer to anything. We dig more trenches and let the old ones collapse in on themselves. Then we wait till it gets dark and Corporal Moody decides whose turn it is to go over the top. Ten at a time. Ten more standing on the ladder. Ten more on the base of the trench. No point complaining. Sometimes I think it would be easier if

'Alfie! Answer the door, will you? If it's the milkman, tell him I'll pay him next week!'

They sent me over as a stretcher bearer last night, love. On account of how I cheeked the sergeant. He's not right in the head, that one, if you ask me. I brought back six bodies – rotten to look at, they were. But I brought them back and managed to survive it. There's only one in five stretcher bearers make it through the night. They usually send the conchies over, not us. I brought one lad back, Margie, and put him with the other bodies. They were piled up together like sacks of rubbish. It was only as I walked away that I saw one of his eyes open. I nearly shouted out with

'Alfie! Tea's ready. Where are you, are you upstairs? Don't let it get cold!'

There's all sorts going on out here now, Margie. Eight different battalions all mixed together. Something happened a few days ago, a bad business in one of the

German trenches. Some of our lot captured it and four soldiers were told to stay there and keep it safe. When we got back it turned out there'd been a German boy still alive and they'd shot him. And now all hell's broken out about the rights and wrongs of it. One lad says it's a damn shame and he wants the sergeant to do something about it. The others say it doesn't matter, that this is going on all the time, so where's the difference? I don't know. Seems to me if he was alone and unarmed they should have taken him in. There's rules, isn't there, and

'Alfie!'

Georgie had stopped writing altogether a year ago. Either that or Margie had found somewhere else to hide his letters, although Alfie didn't think that was the case because he'd searched everywhere. The very last letter stashed under her mattress was the most confusing of all. Alfie had read it so many times, he could have recited it from memory, but still, none of the words or sentences made much sense to him.

. . . going to get out of here, am I? They're everywhere, they are. Eating at my feet. My legs are sore. Bonzo Daly left the tarpaulin off the milk churns and the birds got at them. Stop now stop now. You heard that one, didn't you, Margie, if you were the only girl in the world and I was the only boy. What is he now, eight? He must be all grown up. Wouldn't recognize him. We shot him, didn't

we, on account of how he was complaining about everything. I didn't want any part of it but the sergeant said I had no choice or I'd be court-martialled too. The look on Sadler's face afterwards! Made me laugh, it did. Nothing else would matter in the world today. Stay where you are and then leave – that's what he says over and over. Stay where you are and then leave. Makes no sense. We could go on loving in the same old way. Can't sleep, can I? All your fault, all your bloody fault. This headache won't go. What was it that Wells sang that night? If you were the only Boche in the trench and I had the only bomb... Help me, Margie, can't you. Help me. They said it'd be over by Christmas. They just didn't say which Christmas. Everywhere I look all I can see is

And then there were no more letters and everything went quiet.

Margie had baked a cake for Alfie's ninth birthday. He didn't know where she'd found the flour or the cream, but somehow she'd got hold of them. He'd heard that Mrs Bessworth from the corner shop at Damley Park had an in with the black market. Granny Summerfield came for tea, and so did Old Bill Hemperton, just like they had four years earlier when the war broke out. Kalena and Mr Janáček were missing, of course. No one seemed much in the mood to celebrate. When Alfie read his birthday card it said: *Happy birthday Alfie! Love from Mum and Dad.* Joe Patience put a quarter pound of apple drops through the letter box and no one knew where he had found them; Granny Summerfield wanted Alfie to throw them away but Margie insisted that he be allowed to keep them.

'What are you doing?' he asked his mother that night when everyone had gone home again. Margie was sitting by the gas light with a basket of clothes and she was holding a shirt close to her face as her sewing needle went in and out and in again.

'What does it look like I'm doing? I'm sewing.'

'Whose clothes are they?'

'Not ours, that's for sure. Have you seen the quality of them?' She held the shirt up for Alfie to feel but he shook his head.

'Whose clothes are they?' he repeated.

'Oh, you don't know her,' she said. 'Her name's Mrs Emberg. She's a friend of Mrs Gawdley-Smith's. Very well-to-do. She said she'd give me a shilling for every basket I do. Every ha'penny helps, Alfie.'

'So you're working day and night as a Queen's Nurse, you're taking in laundry, and now you're doing sewing for some rich lady too,' said Alfie.

'Oh Alfie.'

'Mum, where's Dad?'

Margie dropped her needle on the floor and it made a tinny sound as it hit the stonework of the fireplace. She didn't have a shift at the hospital that night; she'd swapped with one of the other girls for Alfie's birthday.

'You know where he is,' she said. 'What do you want to go asking a silly question like that for?'

'Tell me the truth this time.'

Margie didn't say anything for a few moments, but she picked up her needle and held the half-finished shirt in front of her. 'I've to finish six of these by the end of the month,' she said, shaking her head. 'This one's not bad, is it? I told you I always wanted to find something I was good at. Maybe this is it. I'm in a race with Granny Summerfield. Do you know, she knitted thirty pairs of socks last month! That's a pair a day. And her with her bad eyesight! I sometimes wonder if she puts it on for effect.'

'Mum!' said Alfie, tugging at her sleeve. 'Where's Dad?'

'He's away at the war, isn't he?' she snapped, turning on him now, her voice growing cold. 'He's away at this blessed war.'

'He never writes any more.'

'He can't at the moment.'

'Why can't he?'

'Because he's fighting.'

'Then how do we know?'

'How do we know what?'

'How do we know that he's all right?'

'Of course he's all right, Alfie. Why wouldn't he be all right?'

'Maybe he's dead.'

And then something terrible happened. Margie threw down her sewing, jumped out of her seat and slapped Alfie, hard, across the face. He blinked in surprise. Neither Georgie nor Margie had ever hit him in his life, not even when he was very small and acting up. He put a hand to his cheek and felt the sting there but didn't make a sound. Nothing like this had happened since that monster Mr Grace had made him hold out his hand six times for Excalibur and smiled while he was beating him, the purple veins in his great drinker's nose pulsating with pleasure.

A moment later, Margie burst into tears. She threw her arms around him and pulled him to her, and he could feel the dampness of her face against his shoulder. 'Oh Alfie,' she said. 'I'm sorry, love. I didn't mean it. I was upset, that's all. I didn't mean it, honest I didn't.'

'Where's Dad?' he asked again, and Margie pulled away, holding him by the shoulders and looking him directly in the face. The flames from the fire showed the streaks of her tears along her cheeks.

'What?' she asked.

'I want to know where Dad is,' he said. 'I want to know why he hasn't written in almost a year.'

'Of course he's written, Alfie,' said Margie nervously.

'Then where are the letters? You used to keep them under your mattress but there haven't been any new ones since—'

'What are you doing looking under my mattress?' cried Margie. 'Snooping in my things? Honestly, Alfie, I should—'

'If he's written, then where are the letters?'

Margie shrugged and looked as if she was trying to think of a good answer. 'I don't know,' she said eventually. 'I must have lost them. I must have thrown them away.'

'I don't believe you,' shouted Alfie. 'You wouldn't do that. I know you wouldn't. Tell me the truth! You keep talking about a secret mission but you never explain it.'

Margie dried her face and sat back on her chair. 'All right,' she said at last. 'He's not fighting any more, you're right. But he doesn't have time to write. A man from the War Office came to see me. They said that your dad was one of the bravest soldiers they'd ever seen so they gave him new orders. He's doing what he can to put an end to the war.'

'What kind of mission is it?' asked Alfie.

'He wouldn't tell me,' said Margie. 'But I'm sure it's very important. Anyway, the point is that until it's finished, your dad isn't allowed to write to us.'

Alfie thought about it. 'When did he come to see you?' he asked.

'Who?'

'The man from the War Office.'

Margie blew her cheeks out a little and looked away from him. 'Oh, I can't remember,' she said. 'It was months ago.'

'And what was his name?'

'I don't remember. What does it matter anyway?'

'Why didn't you tell me that he came?'

'Because I didn't want to worry you. I know how clever you are, Alfie, but you're only nine. And you were only eight then. There are some things that—'

'Did you tell Granny Summerfield?'

'No, of course not.'

'But she's a grown-up.'

Margie looked flustered and stood up, shaking her head. 'Alfie, I'm not going to continue with this conversation. You asked where your father is and I've just told you. He's on a secret mission. Now can we please just leave it there?'

Alfie was happy to leave it there. There was no point asking any more questions because he was absolutely certain that she wouldn't tell him the truth anyway. No man from the War Office had ever called at their house; there might have been lots of secret missions going on but his father wasn't part of any of them, and wherever he was, Margie knew but wasn't willing to say. But Alfie was certain that he would figure it out eventually if he just put it all together one piece at a time.

Between then and now, however, he hadn't got much further in his investigations. No more letters had arrived, and whenever Alfie caught his mother and Granny Summerfield deep in conversation, they always stopped talking and began discussing the weather or how difficult it was to get fresh apples these days.

In fact Alfie came no nearer to understanding where his father might be until that day at King's Cross when he polished the shoes of the military doctor and his papers got scattered across the concourse.

EAST SUFFOLK & IPSWICH HOSPITAL
Summerfield, George.
DOB: 3/5/1887.
Serial no.: 14278.

And that was the moment when Alfie knew that he had been both right and wrong in the things he believed. His dad wasn't on a secret mission. But he wasn't dead either. He wasn't even in France any more.

He was back in England.

In hospital.

7

HELLO, WHO'S YOUR LADY FRIEND?

Margie was surprised to find Alfie sitting up in bed reading when she opened his bedroom door, but he'd already been awake for almost an hour.

'Are you all right?' she asked, checking his forehead for a temperature. 'You're not sickening for something, are you?'

'I'm fine,' said Alfie. 'I just woke up early, that's all.'

'Well, what's seldom is wonderful.' She looked around and sniffed the air with a frown. 'Why does it always smell of shoe polish in here? It makes no sense when your shoes are always so scruffy. Anyway, your breakfast is downstairs on the table. I'm going to pick up a bit of chicken for our tea this evening. I heard of a butcher on Pentonville Road who might be getting a delivery today. That's the whisper anyway. He's the brother of one of the Queen's Nurses down on Surgical Two and he's promised to put a bit aside for us.'

'Chicken?' asked Alfie, raising an eyebrow in surprise. 'Doesn't that cost a lot of money?'

'There was a bit more in my purse this morning than I expected,' said Margie, giving him a quick wink. 'Funny how that's always happening to me. Do you know, I managed to pay almost all our bills *and* the rent this week? And the good news is that I'm not working tonight so we can stay in, just the two of us, and eat together.'

Alfie frowned. On any other day he would have been pleased by this news, but today he wasn't sure if it was for the best. After all, he didn't know what time he would be home. He had plans. Serious plans. A secret mission of his own.

'Oh,' he said, looking away so Margie would not be able to tell that he was lying, 'but I told Granny that I'd go over to her house for tea.'

'She never mentioned it.'

'Maybe she forgot. Like when she forgot to tell you that she liked that new dress you wore last week.'

'That wasn't forgetfulness,' said Margie, rolling her eyes. 'She said that I shouldn't accept charity from Mrs Gawdley-Smith but if she was only going to throw it out and was happy for me to take it, then why shouldn't I have it? I can't go round in rags for ever, can I? Anyway, beggars can't be choosers.'

'We're not beggars,' said Alfie.

'That's what your granny said. But we're still perilously close to penury, Alfie. Perilously close to penury.' Margie seemed to love this phrase. 'Anyway, can't you tell her you'll go another day? It's not often I'm here in the evening.'

'I'll ask her,' said Alfie, pulling the sheets back now and getting out of bed. 'But if I'm not here when you get home, it means that she got upset and I had to stay.'

'All right, then,' said Margie. 'Well, do your best and hopefully I'll see you later.'

She left the bedroom and Alfie heard her sweeping the hallway before leaving for work. He felt a bit guilty for making her sad but it was for a good reason, he was certain of that. He ran out to the landing, charged down the stairs, out to the privy at the end of the garden, then back inside before the cold could freeze his fingers and toes off, and upstairs to his room, where he took his bag of coins from the back of the sock drawer and poured the contents out onto the sheets.

He counted his money. He'd been saving ever since becoming a shoeshine boy and there was almost eight shillings there now. Eight shillings! He'd never counted it before because he worried that if he knew how much he had then he might go a bit mad and spend it all. But he'd always felt that the day would come when he would need this money; he just didn't know when that day might arrive, or why. And the day was finally here.

Downstairs, he ate his breakfast, had a quick wash at the kitchen sink and made sure that his hair was neatly combed. There was less chance that anyone would stop him if he looked like a respectable little boy. Satisfied, he put his shoes on, slipped a handful of change into his pocket and left the house.

As he walked down Damley Road he noticed Joe Patience smoking a cigarette in his doorway just as an army van came round the corner. Alfie froze. He glanced over at Joe, who looked back at him with an empty expression on his face, but then his eyes, like Alfie's, watched the car as it began to slow down and all the curtains along the street started to twitch. In a moment, the doors opened one by one and the women came out, looking at each other in fear, their faces pale and white as Joe stepped back into his hallway, the door still open, but out of sight of his neighbours.

Not me, they were all thinking.

Please God, not me.

Not today.

The car stopped in front of Alfie, the window rolled down and an officer stared at him as he pressed himself back against the wall.

'Is this Damley Avenue?' the man asked, and Alfie gave a sigh of relief. He only wanted directions.

'Damley Road,' he replied, the words getting caught a little in his throat.

'What's that, son?'

'Damley Road,' he repeated. 'For the avenue, you need to go down the end of the street, turn left, then take the first right. You can't miss it.'

The man nodded, rolled the window up again, and the car drove off as the women went back inside, leaving only Alfie and Joe Patience looking at each other.

'We live to fight another day,' said Joe, smiling the kind of smile that wasn't a real smile at all. Alfie noticed that one of his front teeth had been knocked out and he had a black eye that wasn't really a black eye at all; it was more of a purple, green and yellow eye. 'All right, Alfie?' he asked.

'All right, Joe.'

'You wanna know, don't you? You wanna know what they done to me? My own fault for answering my door after dark.'

Alfie stared at him. He didn't know what Joe meant but he didn't have time to find out. He had a busy day ahead of him. He shook his head quickly and ran down the street, turned right and made his way towards King's Cross.

He got there more quickly than usual because he wasn't weighed down by his shoeshine box, which always seemed to grow much heavier halfway between home and work, and when he reached the station he glanced towards his usual spot, which was empty now, but standing next to it looking around was Mr Podgett, the banker whose son Billy hoped that the war would never come to an end. He was looking at his watch, probably waiting for a shoeshine, but a moment later he gave up and disappeared into the crowd. Alfie marched over to the ticket counter, which was higher than his head, and waited his turn.

'How much to Suffolk?' he asked, unable to see the person behind the counter.

'Who's that?' came a woman's voice, and he repeated his question.

'Lad wants to know how much for a ticket to Suffolk,' said the man in the queue behind him. 'He's too short to see you, isn't he?'

'Thru'pence one way, fivepence return, open all day,' said the disembodied voice, and Alfie reached into his pocket, carefully took out one penny, two ha'pennies and twelve farthings and reached his hand over the top to drop the money in.

'Saints alive,' said the woman's voice.

Still, she swept the money up and he heard the sound of a machine twisting into action; a moment later a ticket fell into the slot and he reached in to take it.

'You want to grow a little taller, sonny,' said the man behind him as he turned away. 'It makes it all easier in the end.'

Alfie felt like sticking his tongue out at him but decided against it; that was the kind of thing children did, and today he was not a child but a grown-up. On account of the fact that he was going to do a very grown-up thing.

He looked up at the station information board but couldn't find any train whose destination was Suffolk. But then he saw one going to Ipswich, leaving from platform two in a few minutes' time, and he made his way over there and stared at it, uncertain whether or not he should risk it. But the hospital, after all, was called the East Suffolk and *Ipswich* Hospital.

'On or off?' said a conductor, tapping him on the shoulder as he glanced at his watch. 'Look lively, lad. She leaves in a minute or two.'

'On,' said Alfie, taking a chance and jumping aboard.

Alfie had never been on a train before, and despite the importance of his mission – his secret mission – he couldn't help but feel a bit excited to be sitting in a carriage waiting for the conductor to blow his whistle and the train to get moving. He remembered his dad telling him how he had thought about working on the trains himself before he got his job in the dairy, and he wondered whether things might have been different if he had. He had read in the newspaper one day that some 'essential service people' were allowed to escape conscription if they provided 'valuable support on the Home Front', and he knew that train drivers and conductors were part of this elite group. But then he remembered that his dad hadn't been conscripted anyway, he'd volunteered, so it wouldn't have made much difference in the end.

A few minutes later the train started to move, and Alfie watched out of the window as it picked up speed and made its way along the track. It was, he decided, the most exciting thing that had ever happened to him – *ever*, in his whole life. He watched the scenery moving past for a long time, until his neck started to hurt, and then he turned round, noticing for the first time the young woman in the carriage with him. She was sitting across from him, but not by the window, reading a book called *The Extraordinary Nature of the Human Mind* by Dr F. R. Hutchison. Alfie wasn't sure how the second word in the title was pronounced and tried sounding it out with his lips. After a moment the young woman turned and stared directly at him.

'Are you quite all right?' she asked.

'Yes, thanks,' said Alfie, turning away in embarrassment and looking out of the window again. He could feel her eyes boring into him.

'Don't you have something of your own to read or are you just going to stare at my book for the entire journey?'

Alfie said nothing. He wished that he had brought *Robinson Crusoe* with him.

'Are you travelling alone?' she continued after a moment.

He turned back to her, swallowing nervously, and then nodded.

'Astonishing,' she declared. 'What age are you anyway, ten?'

'Nine,' said Alfie, flattered beyond his wildest dreams. She thought he was ten! That was an absolute triumph.

'And they let boys of nine travel the railways alone, do they? It wouldn't have happened when I was a girl, let me tell you. I remember my brother Will ran off on a train one day and—' She stopped herself and shrugged her shoulders. 'Yes, well,' she said. 'That was all a long time ago now. I'm sure you don't want to hear about it.'

'How old was he?' asked Alfie.

'How old was who?'

'Your brother. When he took the train alone?'

'A few years older than you, if I remember right. Fourteen or fifteen, I should say. He took a notion to go to London for the day. Came home in his cups and reeking of ladies' perfume. There was an awful fuss. I remember him sitting in my father's armchair as my parents read him the riot act and all he could do was giggle. I thought it was the funniest thing I'd ever seen.' She laughed and looked away for a moment, lost in her thoughts, before opening her eyes wide, blinking them furiously a few times, and then looking back at him, smiling.

'I expect you don't have any plans like that, do you?' she asked. 'You're rather young for that sort of depravity. What's your name anyway?'

'Alfie Summerfield,' said Alfie.

'Mine's Marian Bancroft,' said the young woman. 'You can call me Marian if you like. I don't stand on ceremony. Or Miss Bancroft, if it makes you feel more comfortable. It's a pleasure.' She reached her hand out and Alfie stared at it, uncertain what he was expected to do next. 'Haven't you ever been told that it's rude not to accept an outstretched hand?'

Alfie extended his hand now too and shook Miss Bancroft's. No grown-up had ever asked him to do this before, but of course he had seen it happen a thousand times.

'Very good,' she said, nodding in approval. 'Where are you going anyway?'

'Suffolk,' he replied.

'You know this train is for Ipswich, don't you? But it's so slow I'll be an old lady before we arrive. It was easier of course when the train went from Liverpool Street, but since the bombings everything's been diverted and you never know where you're supposed to go to catch the train you need.

Everything keeps changing and the station attendants are worse than useless. One might as well ask a rabbit for information. Do you know, I've already been to Paddington and Victoria today before I finally discovered that I should be at King's Cross. Still, one shouldn't complain, I suppose. That was a dreadful business.'

Alfie nodded. He remembered reading about this in the newspaper the previous year. A squadron of German Gotha planes had dropped bombs on Liverpool Street Station, killing and injuring a huge amount of people. The mother of one of the boys in his class had been killed, as had the headmaster's brother, Maxwell. A total of 162 dead. More than 400 injured. *More names and numbers*, Alfie thought.

'Would you care for a sweetie?' asked Marian, reaching into her bag and withdrawing a white paper bag of apple drops and handing them across. They were all stuck together and Alfie had to pull at two in order to separate them. 'Oh, take them both,' said Marian, waving a hand in the air. 'Take three. Take them all if you like. I've had too many as it is, but then, I'm addicted to them. I'll turn into an apple drop if I'm not careful. I think I must be the only person in England who's putting on weight during the war. Everyone else looks positively malnourished.'

Alfie took two, popped the first in his mouth

and put the other in his pocket for later.

'It'll get all furry in there,' said Marian with a frown. 'You'll have to wash it before you eat it or you'll come down with something.'

Alfie nodded. Back when Mr Janáček still had his sweet shop, Georgie used to buy him a quarter of apple drops every Saturday morning when he went for his newspaper. He'd come back with the paper folded in half, and Alfie would stand there grinning at him until he opened it up – 'Look what I've got for you,' he'd say – and revealed the package contained inside.

'Ipswich is quite close to Suffolk, of course,' continued Marian, 'so you're probably on the right one after all. Did you speak with a conductor?'

'Yes,' said Alfie.

'Did you tell him where you wanted to go?'

'No.'

'Well, that's where you made your mistake, you see. There's no point boarding a train unless you're absolutely certain that your destinations match. Doing it your way is what lands a person in Edinburgh when they had designs on Cornwall. Are you enjoying your sweetie? You're making a tremendous noise with it. Learn to suck without making that horrible chewing sound – you'll prove far more popular with travelling companions.'

Alfie was uncertain how he could eat any more quietly, and swallowed the entire thing in one go, which made an awful gulping sound, which in turn made Marian narrow her eyes at him as if she was considering switching carriages (which he rather hoped she would).

'What's in Suffolk anyway?' she asked. 'Do you have a sweetheart there?'

'No,' said Alfie, blushing furiously.

'I'm only teasing. Sweethearts are more trouble than they're worth, if you ask me. Mine threw me over, but you don't want to hear about him, do you? But do tell me, what brings you out there?'

Alfie thought about it. He hadn't planned on revealing his secret mission to anyone; not Margie, Old Bill Hemperton, Granny Summerfield or Joe Patience. But he didn't think it could do much harm to tell a stranger, particularly when she seemed to know everything about everything.

'The East Suffolk and Ipswich Hospital,' he said quietly.

'Oh,' she replied, opening her eyes wide in surprise. 'The East Suffolk? Why, that's where I'm going too! What a coincidence! Or perhaps it's not, since we're clearly heading in the same direction. But why on earth is a boy your age going to the East Suffolk? Are you a young genius who became a doctor at the age of five?'

'I'm just visiting,' he said.

'Just visiting? Queer sort of place to go on a visit, but all right, I won't ask any questions. Tell me what you want, keep the rest to yourself. Doesn't matter to me much. I have to attend a lecture there, if you can believe it. Frightful bore. But terribly interesting, of course,' she added, a contradiction that didn't make a lot of sense to Alfie.

'What sort of a lecture?' he asked.

She shrugged, reached inside her bag for a packet of cigarettes and took one out, lighting up in a quick fluid movement of thumb, wrist and flint. When the smoke appeared before her in a sudden haze, she used her other hand to wave it away. 'Awful things,' she said. 'Don't ever start. They take over one's soul. Are you really interested in my lecture or are you just being polite?'

'I'm just being polite,' said Alfie.

'Oh, all right, then. Well, I'll tell you anyway since you asked. I work with soldiers who've come back from the Front, you see. You know about the Front, don't you? Everyone does, I suppose. You'd have to be living under a rock not to. Well, they come back in a terrible way, some of them. So we do what we can to help. I'm doing a sort of triangle, if that makes sense. I live in Norwich, I took the train to London yesterday to visit a friend – an awful girl I used to go to school with and who's now a big voice in the Suffrage movement – have you heard of the Suffrage movement? No, I expect you're too young, but if anyone ever asks, you're in favour of it, all right? – anyway, I took the train down there and now I'm on a train to Ipswich for this lecture. A chap from a hospital in Manchester is giving it. He gave one two months ago, which I attended, and half the men there fell asleep. The women didn't. We paid attention, you see. What's the point of going and not listening? Then tonight I'll head home to Norwich. My father's a vicar there. Don't laugh.'

Alfie shook his head. He had no idea why she thought he might laugh. She hadn't said anything funny.

'I can take you to the hospital, if you like,' she said. 'When we arrive, I mean. It's not far from the station, but if you don't know where you're going you're likely to get lost. And I can't have it on my conscience that I let a ten-year-old boy wander the streets without any idea of his destination.'

'I'm nine,' said Alfie for the second time.

'Well, you'll be ten soon enough, I imagine. Nine-year-old boys usually turn ten at some point. It's the nineteen-year-olds who have difficulty turning twenty.' She looked away and stared out of the window for a few moments, blinking furiously, then closing her eyes and breathing heavily through her nose. Finally she turned back and offered something like a smile. 'Anyway, if you get lost in Ipswich you might have a birthday before you find your way home again. So are we agreed? You'll let me show you the way?'

Alfie nodded, feeling quite exhausted by the way the young woman had talked to him. He felt as if a little nap might be in order and leaned back against the seat, turning his head to look out at the passing fields.

'Oh, we're finished talking now, are we?' asked Marian, and Alfie turned back to her but she shook her head. 'I'm only teasing. Go ahead. Watch the scenery pass. I'm perfectly happy with my own company and that of Dr F. R. Hutchison. If you fall asleep, I'll wake you when we get there. It'll be at least two hours yet. Probably more. The trains take for ever these days. No need to worry.'

Alfie nodded, sat back and closed his eyes. He didn't really want to fall asleep but he thought that if he listened to the young woman talking for much longer, he might go a little mad. He'd never heard anyone speak so fast or have so much to say. He gave a little yawn and was just reflecting that forty winks might come in very useful when a thought occurred to him and he opened his eyes again and sat up straight.

'The hospital we're going to,' he asked. 'What sort of hospital is it, anyway?'

'Well, one for sick people, of course,' said Marian.

'Yes, but what sort of sick people?'

'Sick soldiers. The ones who survived but aren't doing a terribly good job at surviving, if that makes

8

ARE WE DOWNHEARTED?

No other passengers left the train at Ipswich, and Alfie looked around, surprised by the station, which didn't seem like a station at all; there was no seating area, for one thing, no ticket counters and no shoeshine boys waiting for customers. The train had simply stopped and let Marian and Alfie climb off.

'Of course, this isn't the real stop,' said Marian, noticing the bewildered expression on the boy's face. 'But most of the trains don't pull into the real stations any more so there's less risk of bombing. They stop near or nearabouts and one has to walk the rest of the way. It's actually quite convenient for us, though, because the hospital isn't far from here.'

'But how does anyone know where to board?' asked Alfie.

'They just know,' replied Marian with a shrug. 'Word spreads. And if you don't know, then you just keep going to the next stop, wherever that might be.'

A narrow lane bordered by hedges guided them towards a crossroads, and from there three separate paths led in different directions with no signposts to indicate which way they should go next.

'They've all been taken down,' explained Marian. 'There's scarcely a signpost left in England, or haven't you noticed? We don't want any infiltrators to find their way about, you see. There are spies everywhere, or so we're told. I'm not convinced, but who listens to me? Lucky I have a good sense of direction. I might have been a bloodhound in another life.'

She chose the path to their immediate right and kept up a good pace, chattering away about this and that as Alfie ran to keep up with her. She was right, though: it wasn't far to the hospital, and within a few minutes the broken stones sprouting with grass and weeds beneath their feet gave way to a more conventional road, and in front of them, finally, stood the East Suffolk and Ipswich Hospital.

Alfie felt apprehensive as he stared at the imposing walls that ran around the grounds, the long driveway that led to the main hospital, and the enormous pale yellow-brick building itself, which looked more like a castle than anything else.

'Are you quite all right?' asked Marian.

'Yes.'

'You're sure you want to be here? There'll be another train heading back to London quite soon, you know. You could just go back to where we got off and start waving your arms around like a lunatic when you see one coming into sight. It would certainly stop for you. Well, probably anyway.'

'I'm sure.'

'Shall we go up together, then?' she asked. 'There's no point standing here and staring at it like it's a picture postcard.'

'I think I might wait here for a little bit,' replied Alfie, holding back, feeling that it might be best if they parted company now.

'Nonsense, I can't leave you here all alone! Aren't you going to tell me who you're visiting anyway? Perhaps we can find a nurse or someone to help you out.'

'I'd prefer to go up on my own,' said Alfie. 'Thank you, though.'

Marian glanced at her watch. 'Well, if you're absolutely certain,' she said. 'It's up to you, of course. But you'll have to find your own way back to the station later. You remember the way we came? All right, then.'

She extended her hand once again, and this time Alfie shook it without having to be told. 'Very good,' she said, nodding firmly before turning her back on him and marching up the drive.

He watched her for a while before stepping closer to one of the gate posts so that anyone looking out of the hospital beyond would not be able to see him. He didn't want to be spotted in case he was turned away, despite the fact that he wasn't entirely sure what his next move should be. He hadn't really planned things any further than getting to the hospital, and after that . . . well, it was impossible to know. But there was really only one thing for it: he had to go inside.

Alfie began to make his way up the driveway, feeling rather conspicuous; a small boy arriving alone in short trousers, a woolly jumper and a cap, after all, was obviously neither a doctor, a patient nor a student arriving for the lecture.

The path itself was very well kept and separated two wide fields on either side with a straight line that led to the hospital entrance. The lawns were carefully tended, although there were no flowers anywhere in sight. Instead the grass had that strange striped look that lawns in country houses often have, where it appears as if one strip of grass is leaning one way while the other is leaning in the opposite direction.

When he reached the top of the drive, he stopped in front of a grand portico that led to a pair of open oak doors, hiding behind a pillar as he considered his next move. Two young women came out in uniforms completely different to Margie's – they didn't look quite so formal and their blouses were much looser at the neck – and stood in the fresh air, smoking cigarettes, oblivious to his presence behind them.

'And where was Doctor Ridgewell when all this was happening?' asked the first girl.

'Where do you think he was?' replied the second. 'Sitting in his office, head down. Keeping out of the way.'

'And he didn't even come out to speak to her?'

'He had no choice in the end. She said that she wouldn't leave until he did, that they could call the police for all she cared. When he came out at last, you should have seen the expression on his face! Furious, he was! *What are you causing such a fuss for?* he asked her.'

'And what did she say?'

'*For the best reason in the world. For love.*'

Alfie gasped and put a hand to his mouth in surprise. This was the same expression that Mr Janáček always used when he explained why he had moved from Prague to London.

'Poor woman,' said the first nurse, exhaling deeply and shaking her head. 'She's devoted to him, isn't she?'

'Well, of course she is. He's her husband.

You'd do anything for your Frank, wouldn't you?'

'Probably, yes. But look, I know it's a terrible thing to say, but there are times when I'm grateful he was injured early on. It kept him away from the worst of it. It gets him down, of course, not being able to do his bit any more, but I say to him, *Frank*, I say, *you want to see what these poor boys are like out here at the East Suffolk. You want to count your blessings, Frank.* I don't hold back, Elsie. He needs telling sometimes.'

'How's his walking now?'

'Not good.'

'And his spirits?'

'Even worse.'

Alfie slipped round to the other side of the pillars so they wouldn't notice him, and then, while their backs were still turned, he ran into the lobby, where a set of glass doors awaited him, through which he could make out movement in a corridor beyond. Three more nurses were walking in and out of rooms on either side of the hall while a fourth was deep in conversation with a much older doctor who had a white beard and looked a little like Santa Claus. While their attention was diverted, Alfie opened the doors, ran through, and slipped into the first room on his left.

The first thing he noticed in the hospital was the smell. A mixture of cleaning fluids, perspiration, blood and who knew what else. Something foul. It pervaded the air and made him want to gag, but instead he put a hand over his nose until he could grow accustomed to it.

Looking around, he thought he was in an office of some sort. There was a table in the centre of the room, and on it stood a few empty mugs and a teapot with a knitted cosy on top. Hanging over the side of a chair was an apron with a map of Ireland on it and the words A GIFT FROM SKIBBEREEN underneath. A tearoom, Alfie decided. Not an office. Somewhere the nurses came to take their breaks. A sound to his left made him turn and he noticed a kettle on the stove with steam starting to rise through its spout. The moment it began to whistle he gasped, knowing he had only a few seconds before someone appeared and discovered him. Running back out into the corridor, he made his way a little further along, trying to ignore the faint echo of moaning in the air, a noise that was difficult to decipher; it sounded as if a hundred people were in distress behind these doors. He ducked into another room, this time on the right-hand side of the hall, just as he heard footsteps running down to where he had come from.

Closing the door behind him, he turned round with his eyes closed in relief, and exhaled.

When he opened them again, he saw that he was in a bedroom. A man was lying in bed next to an open window, sitting up, his pyjama top unbuttoned halfway down his chest. He had thin grey hair, although his face did not look so very old. He was staring at Alfie with a terrified expression on his face, his mouth hanging open, his hands pressed to his ears to block out the noise of the whistling kettle, whose scream penetrated even here. Alfie looked at him, aghast, not knowing what to say, and only when the whistling stopped a few moments later did the man take his hands away slowly, very slowly, and let them rest on top of his blanket. He stared down at them then, his mouth still open, before turning to look at Alfie. He was trembling slightly.

In a bed opposite him, a second man was reading a novel. When he got to the end of every page, he ripped it out, crumpled it up and threw it on the floor. There were dozens of pages down there already. Alfie narrowed his eyes to make out the words on the front cover. *Madame Bovary.*

'Where's my mum?' asked the first man, and Alfie turned back and opened his mouth, uncertain what to say. 'Is she outside?' he asked finally. 'She said she'd come this morning.'

'I don't think so,' said Alfie. 'I haven't seen any visitors out there.'

'Here, you,' said the second man, waving an arm in the air as if he was a child in a classroom. He held the book up. 'She has a fancy man, you see.'

'Make it stop, please,' said the first man, bending forward and closing his eyes.

'Make what stop?'

'Her husband doesn't know about him,' laughed the second man. 'She's French, though. And you know what they're like. They'd hop on anything.'

The first man made a sudden lunge forward in the bed and Alfie jumped in fright, pulled open the door, and ran quickly back out into the corridor, where he turned a corner and found himself in a ward where ten beds were lined up, five on either side, each one occupied. The moaning sound had been coming from here; each man seemed to be in terrible pain. Some had bandages all over their heads, some had tubes emerging from their bodies with dark red blood either being put in or taken out of them. He felt his stomach twist in fright and looked at the man in the bed next to him, who had no sheets over his body and was simply lying on top of his mattress, making very slight movements as if he could not bear to be lying down much longer. Alfie stared at him: something wasn't right, but it took him a moment to realize what. The man had no left arm, just a stump that ended above the elbow, and his right leg had been amputated at the knee. Both wounds were exposed and a trolley holding clean dressings stood next to the bed; someone must have been attending to him and got called away. Whoever had answered the kettle's whistle, perhaps? Alfie tried not to stare at the angry, pulpy places where the limbs came to an unnatural end, but it was difficult not to. He could see chaotic stitching, and the skin had been folded in upon itself, leaving a wrinkled knot with something resembling a black nail at the centre. Yellowing bandages surrounded his skull and an eye-patch covered one of his eyes. Alfie looked at him in horror, and the man turned slowly, his one eye blinking as his hand reached out and took hold of Alfie's. The boy gasped, tried to pull away, but the man, despite his injuries, was too strong for him, dragging him closer, hissing something under his breath. Alfie reached a hand out to push himself away from the mattress but it landed on something soft and moving – a bottle filled with some dark yellow fluid that fell over as Alfie's hand touched it, spilling its contents on the floor by his feet – and as he pulled away from the man, he slipped in the liquid and fell to the floor, realizing that he had landed in a puddle of the man's piss, and it was all he could do not to scream out loud as he scrambled to his feet and ran from the room.

His father couldn't be here; it wasn't possible. No one could be in a place like this and not go mad.

Out in the corridor again, he gasped for air,

wondering whether he was going to be sick as he held his wet hands in front of his face before wiping them on his trousers. There was blood there too, he realized – blood from the man's urine. Alfie turned round, desperate to get away from these horrors, and started to walk down another corridor, confused now, disoriented, wondering why he had ever thought it was a good idea to come here at all. His legs felt weak beneath him, the way they did when he had that dream where he couldn't run at all and his feet were like ten-ton weights.

He hoped he might find a door that would take him back outside, but instead the corridor led to a nurses' station and, beyond that, another set of glass doors. He desperately wanted to go through them, but there were two people standing by the station – a young doctor and a nurse – talking in concerned voices. If he went that way they would certainly see him. He crouched low in front of the desk, happy now that he was not tall enough to see over the ticket counter at King's Cross, for this desk was about the same height.

'Which ones?' asked the doctor, who spoke in a very posh voice. 'B wing or C wing?'

'C wing, Doctor,' said the nurse in an Irish accent, and Alfie wondered whether she was the person who had brought the tea towel with the map on it. 'Doctor Edgerton says that all four of them are to get their final assessments this week.'

'But what's the hurry? They have another month of recovery ahead of them at least.'

'They're wanted back,' she said, and although Alfie couldn't see her, he knew that she was shrugging her shoulders. 'It's ridiculous, of course, but I don't see what I can do.'

'*I* can do something,' he insisted, his voice growing angrier.

'Then *do*, Arthur,' she said. 'Those men won't survive another month over there. It's criminal to send them back. My God, if the War Office has no thought for their well being, let them at least consider the other soldiers whose lives will be put in danger by their presence.'

'You're preaching to the converted,' said the doctor irritably. 'Look, leave it with me, all right? I'll do what I can. If I have to kick up a fuss, I will. Now, what about those fellows up on the third floor? What can we do with—'

And this was the moment when Alfie, without any warning, sneezed. He froze, grimacing, hoping against hope that they hadn't heard him, but of course that was impossible. A moment later the doctor and nurse had come round to the front of the desk and were staring down at him.

'What on earth . . . ?' asked the nurse.

'Who are you?' snapped the doctor, who looked

furious to encounter a nine-year-old boy sitting on the floor.

'I got lost,' said Alfie.

'Lost? Lost how? What are you doing here anyway? Speak up, boy!'

Alfie said the first thing that came into his head. 'My father's the milkman,' he told them (which wasn't entirely a lie). 'I've been helping him with his rounds.' (Which was.)

The pair stared at him, then at each other, then back at him.

'The supplies are delivered round the back of the hospital,' said the doctor, turning away. 'As you should know by now. Go back out that way.' He indicated a side door that led to the grounds. 'And don't come back in here again, do you hear me? There are sick men in this hospital. They don't need a child running around, spreading who knows what diseases. By God, you stink as well. You smell as if you've wet yourself. Don't you ever bathe? Get out, for pity's sake!'

Alfie turned on his heel and ran through the door, his heart beating wildly. His cap fell off and he ran back to retrieve it, and for a moment he thought that the nurse was looking at him as if she knew he was lying, but he didn't dare say anything and so turned again and ran back outside.

It was a bright day, surprisingly warm for early

November, and Alfie pulled his cap down low over his eyes to keep the sun out. His hands still stank of piss and he longed to wash them, so when he noticed a fountain in the centre of the lawn, he ran towards it and thrust his hands in the stagnant water, telling himself that however bad they smelled when they came out, it couldn't be any worse than they smelled now. Shaking them dry in the air, he considered the long gravel pathway that ran along the side of the hospital and decided to see where it led.

Arriving at a clump of trees, he stared around the grounds and sighed in frustration. If he turned to his left, he would be heading back towards the drive and the front gates, the train station and London, and his secret mission would end in failure. To his right was the hospital itself, filled with its terrible patients, and nothing in the world could have persuaded him to go back inside. He felt sorry for these wounded soldiers, but they didn't seem human to him somehow; and he wondered why the doctors were not doing more to help them. There hadn't even been a nurse in the ward, or a doctor to help the poor man who had been horrified by the whistle of the kettle. Didn't anyone take care of them? Wasn't it somebody's job to look after them? Was this what it was like in Margie's hospital? He couldn't imagine that his mother would leave patients to suffer as badly as these unfortunate men. If his father really *was* here, then he would never leave him in such misery.

He wanted to be brave and keep searching, but he began to feel a sense of panic at being so far from home. He'd never ventured outside a few square miles of London before, and now he'd taken a train to another county more than two hours away. And the truth was, he felt terrified. He hated this hospital. He hated the building, the horrible smell, the terrible people, the awful groaning. He hated all of it, and just wanted to go home. For some reason, Joe Patience's missing tooth and purple, green and yellow eye came into his mind and he wondered why he hadn't cared about what had happened to his father's oldest friend; why he hadn't asked whether he was all right. Georgie would have stopped; Alfie had just kept on walking.

He turned round and was about to make his way back in the direction he had come from when he caught sight of an opening in the bushes to his left a couple of hundred yards away. The hedges were all as neatly trimmed as the grass, but there was a gap there the width of a doorway that led to another garden beyond, and something – a spirit of exploration, perhaps – made him want to know what it looked like in there.

The gap led to a corridor of hedges that twisted

and turned like a maze. He walked along one, then back up the next before heading down a third. Only when he reached the end did the hedges part completely, leading to a wonderful flower garden, laid out in formal blocks with paths separating the beds and a small pond at the end. And to his surprise and dismay there was another group of men out here – half a dozen of them, seated in large bath chairs at some distance from each other, each one wearing a dressing gown and holding a heavy tartan rug across his knees. One man was quite close to Alfie and the boy looked at him nervously; the furthest was some distance away, his back to him and a sun hat pulled down over his bowed head.

Alfie slipped back in amongst the hedges as a nurse walked between the men, saying a few words to each one before continuing on her way. She disappeared through another opening in the hedges further along, and Alfie stepped out again. A small table stood in the corner; on it were some books, a couple of newspapers, a few apples and a pitcher of water. He walked over and had a look. The front pages had been taken away from the papers so all that was left was some fairly insignificant news about problems with the miners and details of a new education bill that was going through Parliament. There was a picture of King George and Queen Mary at an exhibition, and another of the Prince of Wales giving a speech to a group of nurses. Alfie couldn't help himself. He was thirsty. He took a clean glass, poured himself some water and swallowed it down in one gulp, giving a satisfied '*Aaaah!*' when he was finished.

He turned and looked at the young man seated closest to him, who was watching him carefully. He had greasy black hair that fell low over his forehead, and a stubbly beard. There was something about his face that made Alfie think that this was what Old Bill Hemperton might have looked like when he was Young Bill Hemperton.

'Wh-wh-wh-who are you?' the man asked, stuttering over the words, looking down at the ground as he said them.

'No one,' said Alfie.

'You must be s-s-s-someone,' he said.

Alfie thought about repeating the line about being the milkman's son, but something made him not want to lie to this man, even though it wasn't really a lie, only sort of a lie. 'I'm just . . .' he began. 'I'm just looking for a patient, that's all.'

The man nodded and beckoned him over. Alfie wasn't sure. The man put his hand out and waved the fingers casually. 'Come closer,' he said. This time Alfie stepped over carefully. 'Closer,' repeated the man. Alfie came closer, and again the man said it, in a sort of singsong voice this time. '*Closer!*' By now Alfie's face was almost beside the young man's, and he twisted suddenly in his chair, grabbing the boy's chin in his hand. 'I won't go, do you hear me,' he hissed, his voice low, spit flying from his lips and landing on Alfie's face. 'I won't go. You can't make me. Take one of the others. You can't make me, do you hear?'

Alfie pulled away, gasping, and spun round, looking for the exit, but the hedges all seemed to have grown closer together now and the sun was shining down with such ferocity that he couldn't see what he was doing. He turned round and began to feel dizzy, picking a direction and running. He had to get out. He had to get home. He couldn't stay in this awful place any longer. He ran one way, certain that it would bring him back to where he had started – but no, it only took him to the end of the garden, to the man in the last seat with his head bowed low and the sun hat on. Alfie ran past him, looked ahead; there was no way out. He turned back, and this time he saw the exit in the distance and breathed a sigh of relief, glancing at the man in the bath chair for only a moment as he passed him, but it was long enough for the shock of recognition to hit him, and he turned back and stared.

The man looked up and Alfie gasped.

'Dad!' he said.

Georgie Summerfield was sitting in the bath chair, biting his nails as he looked at his son, his eyes narrowing slightly as if he was uncertain of who he was, before shaking his head and looking down, staring at his slippers. He was thinner than Alfie remembered. His cheekbones were more pronounced, his eyes seemed enormous and his lips were very white, with little flakes of dryness crusted upon them.

'Dad, it's me,' he cried, rushing forward. 'It's Alfie!'

Georgie didn't seem to know him and kept staring at his slippers while shaking his head. He started to mumble, but Alfie couldn't hear the words. He leaned close, but none of it made any sense to him.

'. . . in the last one of course, where they kept the tin pots, who was it, it was Humberside, he was always the best of them, no, maybe not, there was Petey too, they got him in the end, he went down with a ship, that's what I heard, while the rest of us were there doing God knows what. *Stay where you are and then leave*, that's what they told us, over and over – what sense does that make anyway? There was a – what was it? A grapefruit? No, of course not, there weren't any grapefruits there, I'm mistaken—'

'Dad!' cried Alfie, putting his hands on his father's shoulders, which had lost some of the muscle that had been there before. Georgie used to have such strong shoulders from lifting the milk churns. 'Dad, don't you know me? It's me, Alfie!'

Georgie glanced up again but showed no sign of recognition. He smiled and looked back down, seemed as if he was about to start talking again but thought better of it and said nothing at all, sitting there immobile, saying nothing, doing nothing, looking at nothing.

'Dad, please,' whispered Alfie. 'I've come all this way to find you. To save you!'

But Georgie simply sighed. It was as if he couldn't hear him. Alfie stood up and looked around in despair. He studied the other men, but none of them could help him. He'd found his father; he'd come all this way and he'd found him. He wasn't on a secret mission for the Government – that had been a lie. And everyone knew it except him. But what did it matter? Georgie didn't even recognize him any more. He didn't know his own son.

'Dad,' he pleaded.

No response.

'Dad!'

He could feel tears forming in his eyes but was determined not to cry. Instead, he stayed rooted to the spot, watching the men rocking back and forth, some of them mumbling to themselves, others not, and then noticed the table with the papers and the water on it once again and had an idea. He ran over, picked up one of the newspapers before folding it in half and reaching into his pocket. Walking back across the garden, he stood in front of his father with the folded newspaper before him, and Georgie looked at the boy, stared at the newspaper, and then back up at his son with a curious expression on his face.

'Look what I've got for you,' said Alfie, opening the paper and showing him the apple drop, the single apple drop that Marian Bancroft had given him in the railway carriage and which he'd put in his pocket for later.

Georgie stared at it, his eyes focusing on this little sphere of green, yellow and red, before the signs of recognition appeared slowly on his face. He swallowed and looked up at his son.

'Alfie,' he said.

9

OH! IT'S A LOVELY WAR!

Alfie rolled his eyes in frustration as he waited for the speech to end. So many people had been crowded together at King's Cross over the last hour that it had become almost impossible to shine any shoes. He was barely even able to keep his usual position between the platforms, the ticket counter and the teashop with all the pushing and shoving that was going on around him. The crowds were listening to a man standing on a tea chest insisting that the war would be coming to an end soon, that no one should give up hope and that it would all be over by Christmas. Most of his audience cheered him on; a few shouted abuse, but they in turn were shouted down by the people standing around them.

Christmas, thought Alfie, shaking his head and grabbing one of his horsehair brushes off the ground before an overweight man in a black suit could stand on it and crush it. *It's always going to be over by Christmas.* But what was it Georgie had said in one of his letters? *They just didn't say which Christmas.*

He pulled his copy of *Robinson Crusoe* out of his pocket and started to read, trying to block out the sounds of the ovations and the jeers that seemed to be coming in equal parts from all around him.

'I tell you now,' roared the man on the tea chest, 'that the sacrifice that all of you have made, that your loved ones have made, will be remembered for ever!' His voice rose on 'for ever', and everyone cheered wildly. 'We will win this war with honour and bring our boys home!' Another cheer, more jostling in the crowd, and this time a woman nearly fell on top of him; she had the rudeness to place both her hands on his head to steady herself. Alfie felt outraged, absolutely outraged. 'Together we will go forward!' continued the man. 'United against tyranny! Firm in our resolve! Victory is within our grasp – the end is nigh – keep steady hearts and minds and we shall bring this conflict to an end without any more loss of blood. Thank you all!'

Everyone whooped and threw their hats in the air – except for one man standing nearby who was shaking his head. He turned and noticed Alfie watching him and said, 'The end is nigh all right.' But Alfie looked away and was pleased to notice that the crowd was finally starting to disperse. He glanced up at the enormous clock over the ticket booth. A quarter past two. There was still time to earn a little money if luck was on his side.

'Shoeshine!' he shouted, trying his best to get as much strength and resolve into his voice as the speaker had so that he might be heard over the dispersing crowds. 'Get your shoeshine here!'

'I believe I'll get my shoes shined, young man,' said a voice behind him, and he turned round to see the speech-maker himself standing there, looking down at him with a smile on his face. He was a tall thin man with a heavy moustache and thick dark hair parted at the side. He looked tired, as if he hadn't had a good night's sleep in a few years, but there was a steely expression in his eyes. He spoke with a strange accent that Alfie didn't fully recognize. 'I have time, don't I?' he asked another man with a briefcase standing next to him, who glanced up at the clock for a moment before nodding.

'A little time,' he said. 'But we need to be at the Palace by three.'

'Plenty of time, then. Plenty of time,' he replied, sitting down opposite Alfie on the customers' chair. 'You go get yourself a cup of tea, Rhodhri, and leave me and the boy to our chat. It's not often I get to speak to one of the young people. What's your name, lad?'

'Alfie,' said Alfie.

'That's a fine name, that is,' said the man, nodding his head wisely. 'I had a friend called Alfie when I was a boy. He had six spaniels, and he called them Alfie the First, Alfie the Second, Alfie the Third, and so on, as if they were kings.'

'Hmm,' said Alfie, thinking this was rather ridiculous. There had only been one King Alfred, as far as he knew. Alfred the Great. He liked the sound of that. *Alfie the Great!*

'Anyway, down to business, lad,' said the man. 'A nice shiny tip, if you please, take the dust off the sides and do something to get rid of the scuffs on the heels. Don't be shy with the polish either.'

Alfie nodded and took out his brushes and jars, settling the man's left shoe on the footrest.

'Perhaps I shouldn't ask this,' the man said after a moment, 'but shouldn't you be in school today? Or maybe all the London schools have closed down and no one has had the good grace to tell me!'

'I was sick, sir,' said Alfie.

'Then what are you doing here?'

'I mean, my teacher was sick. So we were given a half-day's holiday.'

'I don't believe a word of it. But we won't fall out over a little white lie. At least you're here earning a living for your family and not wasting your time on the streets doing nothing. You do give your earnings to your mother, I hope?'

'I do, sir, yes,' replied Alfie, neglecting to mention that he had kept some of it back for his secret mission and was keeping even more back now for secret mission part two, which was going to take even more planning than the first one but was infinitely more important. And considerably more dangerous.

'Good boy. You give a quality shine too, I'll give you that,' the man added, looking down at the way Alfie's hands moved quickly over his shoes, adding just the right amount of polish here, clearing a bit of dirt away there, the dusters and brushes moving as if independently of his hands. 'You must have been at this a while. A right little professional, aren't you?'

'Thank you, sir,' said Alfie, tapping the tip of the left shoe with his fingers to indicate that it was done. The man took his foot down and replaced it with the other one, and Alfie got to work again.

'My cousin Thomas used to shine shoes at the train station in Llanystumdwy,' said the man, taking a pipe from his pocket and lighting it up, waiting a moment to allow the flame from the match to connect with the fug in the bowl. 'Funny fellow, he was. Wouldn't get a haircut on account of the fact that he was afraid of the barber's scissors. Believed he had nerve endings in his hair, see. That was a long time ago now, of course. It's pleasant just to sit here, though. I don't get a lot of time to sit around doing nothing.'

'You have a job then, sir?' asked Alfie, who assumed the man was unemployed if he could afford to stand around train stations in the middle of the day, making a show of himself.

'Oh, I do, I do,' said the man.

'Giving speeches?' asked Alfie.

'Amongst other things. Politics should be about doing things, though, not just *talking* about doing things, don't you agree? But if you don't get out among the people, then they start to think that you've forgotten them and they look around to see whether someone else might do a better job. Do you know who told me that?'

'No, sir.'

'The King,' he replied with a smile. 'He makes the occasional remark that's worth remembering. There was one last year too. I wrote it down somewhere. He's due another any day now. We live in hope, anyway.'

Alfie stopped what he was doing and looked up in astonishment. 'Have you really met the King?' he asked.

'Of course. Many times. I see him two or three afternoons a week at least. I have a meeting with him in about half an hour, as it happens.'

Alfie smiled and shook his head. He came across all sorts of strange folk in this job, and even though the man seemed respectable enough, he was obviously mad or delusional or both. He glanced over towards the station entrance, where a group of men in suits were all standing, smoking and chatting, and then, to his horror, he saw a woman stepping through the centre of them and looking around the station as if she was lost.

The very last person Alfie expected to see today.

His mum, Margie.

'Work here every day, do you, lad?' asked the man, and Alfie looked back up at him and blinked.

'I beg your pardon, sir?' he asked.

'I wondered whether you work here every day. You can tell me the truth. I won't be reporting back to the cabinet on it.'

'Four days a week,' said Alfie, who felt somehow that he could trust him not to report him to the headmaster. 'Tuesdays, Wednesdays, Fridays and Saturdays. I go to school on Mondays and Thursdays.'

'And Sundays?'

'I take a rest on Sundays,' said Alfie. He glanced round again and watched as his mother searched in her bag for something; when she looked up, he picked his cap up off the ground, emptied his earnings into the bottom of Mr Janáček's shoeshine box and pulled it low over his head so there was less chance of his being seen.

'You're not the first to do that,' said the man. 'What I wouldn't give for a rest on a Sunday! I would think all my Christmases had come together.'

Alfie dared to look round once more; now his mother was standing in the centre of the concourse staring up at the information board before turning her head to glance at the clock over the ticket booth. And then, before he could look away, she stared in his direction. He looked down quickly, pulling the cap lower still as he continued with his shining. Peering round only a little, his heart sank when he realized that Margie was walking directly towards him, looking as if she couldn't quite believe the evidence of her own eyes. Alfie shook his head, devastated, and waited. He'd been caught. Everything would come out now.

He would never get to complete his secret mission part two.

Georgie would be condemned to that horrible place for ever.

'I don't believe it,' said Margie, standing over him now. 'I saw you over here and wondered whether my eyes were playing tricks on me.'

Alfie reached up to take his cap off, but before he could do so, the man had spoken.

'If you are wondering whether I am who you think I am,' he said, 'then yes, I am.'

'I thought as much,' said Margie. 'I recognize you from the newspapers.'

'David Lloyd George,' said the man, extending his hand.

'Margie Summerfield,' said Margie.

'It's a pleasure, madam.'

Alfie held his breath. Could it be that she had not seen him after all? She was standing right over him, but his cap was pulled well down over his face. She wasn't even looking at the shoeshine boy.

'I wouldn't have thought that the Prime Minister could sit around having his shoes shined in the middle of the afternoon,' said Margie. 'You do know there's a war going on, don't you?'

'I do, Mrs Summerfield, yes,' said the man, his voice growing a little deeper now. 'But even prime ministers are allowed a few minutes to themselves.'

Alfie could scarcely believe his ears. *The Prime Minister?*

'I'm sorry,' said Margie. 'That was rude of me.'

'It's quite all right.'

'I'm just so tired.'

'Please,' he insisted. 'I took no offence. We live in stressful times.'

'May I ask you something?'

'You may.'

Margie didn't hesitate. 'When will this blessed war be over? And please don't say by Christmas. Give me an honest answer. Even if it's not the one I want to hear.'

There was a long pause, and finally Mr Lloyd

George simply sighed and shrugged his shoulders. 'I don't know,' he said. 'Soon, I hope. Very soon. Can I be absolutely honest with you?'

'Yes.'

'It will be over within the week or it will drag on interminably. It depends on various issues which are being resolved at the moment. But I am hopeful, Mrs Summerfield. I remain hopeful. You have a husband fighting over there?'

Margie shook her head. 'Not any more,' she said.

'I'm very sorry.'

'No, you misunderstand me,' said Margie quickly. 'He's not dead. He's in hospital.'

'Wounded?'

'Not physically.'

Another pause. 'Then in what way?' he asked.

'They're calling it shell shock, aren't they?' said Margie, and Alfie's eyes opened wide now. That was the word that Marian Bancroft had used on the train.

'Ah yes,' said Mr Lloyd George. 'Yes, that is indeed what they're calling it. Mr Asquith has spoken to me about this – it's difficult to know what to make of it.' Alfie couldn't believe how ridiculous this conversation had become. Mr Asquith had talked about shell shock? Now he'd heard everything. 'When a man has his legs blown off, the evidence is there before one's eyes. When he says that his mind is destroyed, well . . .' He trailed off.

'You think these men are lying?' asked Margie, the steel evident in her voice now. 'You think they're cowards? That they don't want to fight?'

'Not at all,' he replied. 'I don't know enough about the condition, that's the truth of it.'

'Then perhaps you should find out.'

'Yes,' said Mr Lloyd George. 'Yes, perhaps I should.'

Margie glanced at her watch. 'I better go,' she said. 'I'm visiting my husband in hospital.'

'Which hospital is he in?'

'The East Suffolk and Ipswich.'

'That's a fine place. I wish him a swift recovery.'

'Do something,' said Margie, leaning forward now, so close that if she had just glanced to her left and down a little, she would have locked eyes with her son. 'Do something to end it. Please.'

And with that, she turned away and marched towards the ticket booth, opening her bag as she did so and taking out her purse.

'A distraught woman,' said Mr Lloyd George, sitting down again with a sigh. 'There are so many with loved ones who have been lost or wounded. Tell me about your family, boy. You have brothers? A father?'

'I don't have any brothers,' said Alfie.

'And you never had any?'

Alfie frowned; this seemed like a strange question to ask. But then he realized what the man meant and shook his head. 'No,' he said. 'It's always been just me.'

'And your father?' continued Mr Lloyd George, a note of apprehension creeping into his voice. 'He is keeping well?'

'He's in France,' said Alfie, lying. 'He's over there doing his bit.' A phrase he had heard Old Bill Hemperton say on a hundred occasions.

'I hope he stays safe,' said the Prime Minister. 'You must be proud of him, yes?'

Alfie said nothing, just nodded his head and continued cleaning the Prime Minister's shoes. He looked over towards the ticket booth and twisted a little so that he would be less visible to his mother if she turned round again.

'Are you really the Prime Minister?' he asked after a moment.

Mr Lloyd George nodded. 'I am, lad, yes. If you can believe it. Don't I look like a prime minister, then?'

Alfie considered it. 'I don't know,' he said. 'I don't know what a prime minister is supposed to look like.'

'Picture a man,' said Mr Lloyd George. 'About six feet in height. With a moustache and a pipe. Give him a friendly smile and a Welsh accent.

And there you have it. The very model of a perfect British prime minister.'

Alfie smiled. *Welsh!* Of course, that's what his accent was.

'I have a friend who wants to be Prime Minister,' he said after a moment.

'Oh yes? And what's his name, then?'

'Kalena Janáček. And he's not a he, he's a she.'

Mr Lloyd George burst out laughing and shook his head. 'Don't you mean she'd like to be *married* to the Prime Minister?' he said, and Alfie frowned.

'No,' he said. 'She wants to *be* the Prime Minister. Herself.'

'Well, it's a radical idea,' Lloyd George replied, thinking about it and puffing on his pipe for a moment. 'But we live in an age of radicals, Master Summerfield, so I wouldn't rule anything out. You may tell her that I said that.'

'I don't see her any more,' said Alfie.

'Why not? Did you have a falling out?'

'You took her away,' said Alfie. 'Her and her father. They were sent to the Isle of Man.'

The Prime Minister nodded and considered it. 'Janáček – that's what you said, isn't it? Austrian, were they? Polish?'

'English. She was born three doors down from me.'

'A curious name for an English girl.'

'Her father came here from Prague.'

'So half Austro-Hungarian, half English, then.'

'She wasn't a fraction.'

Mr Lloyd George frowned and looked at the boy with a concerned expression on his face. 'You're a bright one, aren't you?' he said after a long pause. Alfie glanced towards the ticket booth again; Margie was now first in the queue and speaking to the man behind the counter.

'How do they look, sir?' he asked, sitting back and letting the Prime Minister examine his shoes.

'Excellent job, my boy,' he said. 'I'm very grateful. I have an appointment with His Majesty in about twenty minutes and it's important to look one's best when courting royalty. They have the most curious obsessions.' Alfie's eyes opened wide; he found it hard to believe that he had just shone a pair of shoes that would soon be standing before the King. 'Of course, the King's own shoes are always sparkling,' added Mr Lloyd George. 'I think he has a boy on the staff to do it for him. Or a fleet of them. I think he breeds them in-house. Now wouldn't that be a fine position for a lad like you?' he added, smiling, and Alfie felt himself beginning to laugh. It was a fantastical idea. 'Anyway,' he said after a moment. 'How much do I owe you?'

'A penny, sir,' said Alfie, and the Prime Minister reached into his pocket and pulled out three pennies. 'One for you, one for your mother and one to keep your father safe from harm,' he said. 'Ta-ra now, Alfie. Thanks for the shine.'

As he headed back towards his companion, Margie turned away from the ticket counter and Alfie watched as she stared directly into the Prime Minister's face. He was accustomed to being stared at, of course, so he didn't look away but gave her a polite bow and a tip of his hat as he walked on. Alfie moved behind the pillar and watched her as she stared, before shaking her head and walking over to platform two to board her train. Only when she was safely out of sight did Alfie run round to the information chart to find out where her train was going.

He wasn't surprised by the destination he read there: Ipswich.

It was later in the afternoon than Alfie usually stayed by his shoeshine stand but he was determined to wait, for the man usually showed up on Tuesday afternoons. The time passed slowly, but finally his patience was rewarded when he looked up to see the doctor from the East Suffolk and Ipswich Hospital; the same one whose papers had blown around the concourse the week before, marching towards him. He stared at him and swallowed.

'Shoeshine please,' said the man.

Alfie nodded and sat up straight, arranging his materials once again as the man sat down and put his foot on the footrest. 'I remember you, don't I?' he asked. 'You were here last week.'

'I'm here every week, sir,' said Alfie. 'The name's Alfie.'

'Doctor Ridgewell,' said the man.

'Are you a soldier, sir?'

'Of a sort. I was a consultant physician before the war. Now I work in an army hospital.'

'I'd like to be a doctor someday,' said Alfie, even though he had no interest at all in being a doctor. But he knew that grown-ups liked it when boys his age pretended to be interested in their jobs.

'Is that right?' Dr Ridgewell asked, looking pleased. 'Well, I suppose everyone has to start somewhere. Believe it or not, I used to earn my pocket money by making deliveries for our local fishmonger every Saturday. Of course, I was fortunate. My father was a doctor too. As was his before him. But there's a chap at the hospital, Doctor Morehampton, and his father was a coal man, if you can believe it. And another, Doctor Sharpely, who's the son of a greengrocer. So it takes all sorts, I suppose. What does your own father do?'

'He's in the army.'

'Well, of course he is. Quite right too. But what did he do before that?'

'He worked at the dairy down Damley Road,' said Alfie. 'He drove a milk float.'

'A good honest job,' said Dr Ridgewell, nodding, satisfied by the response. 'And I dare say he'll be back at it soon. This war will be over by Christmas, you know. There's no doubt about it now.'

Alfie said nothing.

'What sort of doctor are you?' he asked after a little while, finishing one shoe and switching over to the other.

'What do you mean?'

'Do you look after people if they have a cold? Or if they've broken their leg?'

'It's quite complicated,' said Dr Ridgewell. 'Are you sure you want to know?' Alfie nodded. 'All right, then. I deal with the medicine of the mind. Chaps who've gone a bit do-lally, if you know what I mean. Fellows who aren't playing with a full deck any more. Men who can't see the wood for the trees. Do you see what I'm getting at?'

'I can't say I do,' said Alfie, having no idea what any of that meant.

'Mad men,' explained Dr Ridgewell. 'You know what it is to go mad, don't you?'

'Yes. Sometimes I think I might be going that way myself.'

'Well, then, you know what I'm talking about. I look after those whose minds have gone a bit befuddled.' He tapped the side of his head with his fingers. 'There's a lot of it about these days, of course. These chaps who come back from the trenches. The ones who come back alive, I mean. It's not easy for them, you see. They've seen a lot of terrible things, experienced an awful lot of trauma. It can play havoc with the old reasoning functions.'

'And what happens to them?' asked Alfie, stopping his polishing now and looking up.

'Differs from man to man,' replied Dr Ridgewell. 'Some can't get out of it at all. It's too early to say, of course, but there are some who are probably lost for life. Others might take years to recover. Some just need a good talking to in order to pull them back to their senses. As I say, it differs from man to man. There's no hard and fast rule.'

'Does anyone die?' asked Alfie, frowning.

'Oh dear me, no,' said Dr Ridgewell. 'It's not that sort of disease, you see. Although I suppose there are some who might say it's a living death. Chaps who've gone through so much bombing and shelling and shooting and witnessed so many terrible things that their minds just pack up on them and say to their owners, *You go your way and I'll go mine.* It's a rotten business. But anyway, that's what I do. I try to put these fellows back together again. How are we getting along there? All finished?'

Alfie nodded and took his dusters away. 'As good as new,' he said.

'Capital job too,' said Dr Ridgewell. 'You really

are very good at this, you know. If you decide to go into medicine some day it'll be a great loss to the shoe-shining business!' He stood up and threw a penny into Alfie's cap. 'Well, goodbye for now. See you next week, I expect.'

Yes, thought Alfie as he walked away.

Perhaps.

10

HUSH, HERE COMES A WHIZZ-BANG

The green paint on the front door was beginning to crack and Alfie could make out scars of red peeping through from underneath. He stood before it nervously, uncertain whether or not this was a good idea, but before he could decide, the door opened and there he was, standing before him. Joe Patience. The conchie from number sixteen.

'Alfie,' he said in surprise. 'I thought I heard someone out here. I was starting to get worried. I'm glad it's only you.' He looked outside for a moment, glancing up and down the street to make sure that no one else was there, before stepping back into the hallway.

'Hello, Mr Patience,' said Alfie.

'Mr Patience? It's Joe, you know that. What brings you here anyway? It's a long time since you came knocking on my door.'

'I wanted to ask you something. I need your help.'

Joe raised an eyebrow. The bruising around his eye had got a little better over the last few days; the different colours had settled into a single shade of light blue and it didn't look as tender as before.

'I didn't know who else to ask,' continued Alfie. 'I'm on a secret mission, you see. Well, I *was* on a secret mission, but now I'm on another one.'

Joe frowned and seemed uncertain what he should do, but finally he stepped aside and ushered Alfie in. 'Well, you'd better come in, I suppose,' he said. 'I don't like leaving my front door open for too long anyway.'

It had always seemed strange to Alfie that whenever he went into anyone else's house on Damley Road it felt like being in his own home, only there were so many subtle differences. The rooms were all the same shapes and sizes, the corridors all led in the same directions – or in the mirror images of those directions – but while he was familiar with every stick of furniture in his own house and everything that he, his mother and father owned – their ornaments, their knick-knacks, their cushions – the things he saw in other people's homes were completely alien to him.

He looked around now, and the first thing he noticed about Joe Patience's living room was the number of books on display. The walls were lined with shelves and every spare space was taken up with hard-covered volumes, some in languages that

Alfie didn't even understand. Joe saw the way Alfie was staring around in amazement, his mouth hanging open, and smiled.

'Are you a reader, Alfie?' he asked.

'I like *Robinson Crusoe*,' he replied. 'Mr Janáček gave me a copy for my fifth birthday. I couldn't read it very well then but I've read it three times since. It's the best book ever written.'

'It's a good book, certainly,' said Joe Patience. 'But until you've read a lot more, you should reserve judgement. What other books have you read?'

Alfie shook his head. 'Just storybooks at school. None of them are as good as *Robinson Crusoe*. Have you read all these books?' he asked, wondering how many there were. He leaned back and looked down the corridor, which was also lined with books on both walls, and into the kitchen, where he could see another row above the range. Joe's clarinet was propped up against the kitchen table. He used to play it outside, of course, before the war. The whole street could hear him. Now he only ever played indoors, in private.

'Most of them. There's not much else for me to do these days. Now, are you going to tell me what you're doing here or do I have to guess?'

Alfie stared at Joe, wondering how best to phrase this. He was only the same age as Georgie – thirty-one – but he looked much older. He had heavy bags under his eyes, maybe from reading too much, maybe from a lack of sleep, and a scar running along one of his cheeks. Above his left temple was a piece of very smooth skin where his hair didn't grow. It looked as if he'd been burned badly.

'You know my dad,' said Alfie finally.

'Of course I do,' replied Joe with a quick laugh. 'We grew up together. You know that.'

'And you know the war?'

Joe paused for a moment but then nodded. 'I do,' he repeated.

'Well, when my dad went to the war we used to get letters from him all the time and it seemed like he was having a great time,' said Alfie, feeling the words start to pour out of him now, tumbling over each other as he tried to tell Joe everything he knew. 'Only then the letters stopped coming, or I thought they stopped coming, but actually Mum was keeping them to herself and not letting me see them but I found them anyway – she kept them under her mattress – and I read them and they didn't make a lot of sense, most of them; or they did at the start, when he was telling us about all the terrible things that were happening, but then after a while he stopped talking about those things and everything just got confused.'

'Slow down, slow down,' said Joe, holding a hand up in the air. 'Your dad went to the war, I got that part. If you're worried that he hasn't been in touch – well, the soldiers can't always write. They're fighting, of course, and—'

'My dad's not fighting,' said Alfie, shaking his head.

'He's not?' asked Joe, turning his head away, and Alfie gasped in surprise.

'You know, don't you?' he asked. 'You know about my dad!'

'Know what?'

'You *know*!'

'Alfie, you're not making any sense.'

'My dad's in hospital. A couple of hours from here. He's been there for . . . well, I don't know how long.'

'Ah,' said Joe Patience.

'Only I'm not supposed to know that.'

'So how did you find out?'

'I'm clever,' said Alfie. 'I worked it out. But you knew, didn't you? I can see it in your face.'

Joe nodded his head. 'I did, yes,' he said. 'Well, have you been to see him, Alfie?'

'Yes.'

'Did he recognize you?'

'Eventually. But it wasn't like it was before. He knew me, and then he didn't know me. And then the nurses came out so I had to scarper. But before I did, he shouted something out. The nurses didn't pay any attention, but I did. I heard that word and I know he was shouting it to me.'

'What did he say?' asked Joe.

'*Home.*'

Joe raised an eyebrow, then reached for his cigarettes and lit one up. Alfie had noticed that whenever any grown-up wanted a good think, that's what they did. They reached for the tobacco and their matches.

'Have *you* been to see him?' asked Alfie after a moment.

Joe nodded, taking a long drag from his cigarette. 'I've been once a week, every week,' he said. 'Well, since I got out of prison, that is.'

'Why did you never tell me?'

'Your mum asked me not to. But I suppose, since you know now, there's no point lying about it. What does Margie say about all this?'

'She doesn't know,' admitted Alfie. 'I haven't told her.'

Joe nodded; this didn't seem to surprise him in the least.

'Can I ask you something?' asked Alfie after a long silence.

'Sure,' said Joe with a shrug. 'Ask me anything you want.'

'Why do they call you the conchie from number sixteen?'

Joe frowned. 'Because that's where I live,' he said.

'No,' said Alfie, shaking his head. 'I understand that part. It's the first bit I don't get. What's a conchie?'

Joe smiled a little. 'You don't know what the word means?'

'No.'

Joe nodded. 'It's not really a word at all,' he said. 'It's a shortened version of a word. Like Old Bill Hemperton, everyone calls him Bill but his real name is William. Or like saying kids instead of children.'

'So what's conchie short for, then?' asked Alfie.

'Conscientious objector,' said Joe. 'It means someone who doesn't want to fight in the war for humanitarian, religious or political reasons.'

Alfie frowned and stared down at the carpet, noticing the loops of the pattern and how they intersected with each other. There were a lot of words in that sentence that he didn't understand. He looked up, puzzled.

'At the start,' explained Joe, 'before conscription, men signed up of their own accord. To fight, I mean. Your dad signed up that first day, remember?' Alfie nodded. 'I can see him now, walking down Damley Road in his uniform, looking pleased as punch with himself. I was outside washing my windows. *Georgie,* I said. *You've not gone and signed up, have you? Tell me you haven't.*

'*Fighting for King and country, amn't I?* he told me.

'*For what? What's the King ever done for you?*

'*Nothing so you'd notice. But a man's gotta do . . .* and all that rubbish.

'I remember staring at him, Alfie, as if he'd lost his mind. Lost control of his reason entirely. *You must be mad*, I told him.

'*You say that now, Joe, but your time will come. Watch, you'll have signed up too by the end of the week.*

'*Pigs will be flying over the Houses of Parliament when that day comes, Georgie*, I told him. *I'm not signing up to go killing people. What have the Germans ever done to me anyway? Nothing so as you'd notice.*

'But your dad just laughed and shook his head and said my time would come. I watched him as he went into your house and I wondered what was going on in there. What your mum thought. What you thought.'

'Granny Summerfield said we were finished, we were all finished,' said Alfie.

'And she wasn't far wrong, was she? You want to listen to your granny, Alfie. Some of these old people, they know what's going on. They've seen a thing or two.'

'She doesn't like you very much,' said Alfie quietly.

'She used to. She doesn't understand me, that's all. She's a good woman, though, Alfie. She did a lot for me when I was a kid. She cleaned me up when . . . I mean, she looked out for me after . . .'

'After what?' asked Alfie.

'My old man used to knock me around something awful,' said Joe, looking down and moving his feet around slowly on the carpet. 'Used to knock my old mum around too. Handy with his fists, he was. I was afraid of him, of course. My mum was afraid of him. You know the only person who wasn't afraid of him?'

'Who?'

'Your Granny Summerfield,' said Joe. 'She used to keep me hidden in her wardrobe when he was on the warpath. One time he practically broke down her front door looking for me on account of how I'd forgotten to clear out the muck from the back of the privy, and she took a rolling pin and stood before him, bold as brass and said, *If you don't get out of this house right now, Sam Patience, I'll split your head in two, do you hear me?* And there was something about her that scared him because he left after that. She's a tough old bat, I'll give her that.'

Alfie tried to imagine it. Granny Summerfield facing down a bully!

'And then, when I was your age,' continued Joe, 'she got him to stop hitting us altogether.'

'How did she do that?'

'She organized half a dozen men from Damley

Road and got them to call on my old man. Set him straight about a few things. Tell him what was what. I don't know what they said to him, but he never laid a finger on my mum or me after that. And when he died – hit by a coal man's wagon when he was reeling home, drunk – your granny made sure that my mum and me were taken care of. I know what she thinks of me now, Alfie – I see it in her face whenever she passes me on the street – but I owe that woman a lot. I just wish I could make her understand, that's all.'

'She doesn't like conchies,' said Alfie. 'But then she didn't want Dad to sign up when the war started either. It doesn't make any sense to me.'

'Look, Alfie,' said Joe, putting his cigarette out and lighting another one. 'I didn't agree with what your dad was doing either. I thought he was mad. But I admired him for it. He wasn't thinking about his own well-being. Of course, he wasn't thinking about his family's well-being either, but we'll set that aside for now. Off he went, like so many of the men from around here. There was a fever to join up in 1914, Alfie, a fever. Everyone seemed to think it was just a lark. But at least he survived it. Look at Charlie Slipton from number twenty-one. He didn't last long, did he?'

'He threw a stone at my head once for no reason whatsoever,' said Alfie, who couldn't seem to let this go.

'Maybe he was aiming for something else and missed. Hit you by mistake. Anyway, when conscription came in in 1916 they said that every healthy man between the ages of eighteen and forty-one had to sign up, unless their wives were dead and they had a kid or two to take care of. No say in the matter at all! No right to your own opinion! But that's where the conscientious objectors came in – the conchies, as they call us. There were lots of us, you know. Who stood up and refused to fight.'

'Were you afraid?' asked Alfie.

'Yes!' said Joe, leaning forward and looking the boy directly in the eyes. 'Of course I was afraid. What kind of fool wouldn't be afraid, going over to some foreign country to dig out trenches and to kill as many strangers as you could before some stranger could kill you? Only a lunatic wouldn't be afraid. But it wasn't fear that kept me from going, Alfie. It wasn't because I knew I'd be injured or killed. It was the opposite of that. It was the fact that I didn't want to kill anyone. I wasn't put on this earth to murder my fellow man. I'd grown up with violence – can't you see that? I can't bear it. What my old man did to me . . . it broke something in my head, that's all. But if I went down the street now and hit a man on the head with a hammer, sent him to his Maker, then they'd put me in jail for it. They might even hang me. But because I wouldn't go over to France and do the same thing, they put me in jail anyway. Where's the justice in that, can you tell me? Where's the sense?'

Alfie thought back to that long period when he hadn't seen Joe Patience for almost two years. And then, when he had reappeared on Damley Road, he looked different. He looked older and sadder. And he had all these scars.

'So what happened to you?' asked Alfie.

'They brought me in,' said Joe with a shrug, looking away. 'Put me on trial. Said I was a coward. I got sent to jail. It made a change from being given white feathers everywhere I went anyway.'

Alfie frowned. 'White feathers?' he asked.

'That's what they do. Women, mostly. Men just attack. Women, they hand out white feathers. To any young man they see who isn't in a uniform. It means you're a coward. It's a rotten thing, Alfie, it really is. They come up to you on the street and they're all smiles; they approach you like they're your long-lost friend or some forgotten cousin or a girl you went to school with, or maybe they just like the look of you, and when you stop too they reach into their bags, they don't say a word, and they pull a feather out and press it into your hands. And then they just walk away, bold as brass. They never even open their mouths. And everyone can see what they're doing, the whole street. Everyone looks. They might as well take a hot iron and brand you a coward. It's a horrible thing, Alfie, a horrible thing.'

Alfie remembered the young man whose shoes he'd shined before going to his brother's funeral. He'd mentioned something about this. *A woman came up to me in the middle of Piccadilly Circus. Opened her handbag, and in front of everyone she . . . she . . .*

'And jail?' said Alfie after a moment. 'What was that like?'

'What do you think it was like?' asked Joe. 'They put me in there because I wouldn't fight, and then I spent more time fighting than I'd ever done before. The men inside, they went after me because of my beliefs. Not all of them, of course. There were other conchies there too, and we all got beatings at different times. You see this scar?' Joe indicated the deep ridge on his cheeks and Alfie nodded. 'That was the result of being inside. And this . . .' He pointed towards the burn on his head. 'You don't want to know how this happened or what they did to me. Anyway, when I got out, I didn't know what to do. So I came home. The funny thing is, it's not so bad any more. You might have noticed I have a limp.' Alfie nodded; he *had* noticed. 'Well, that came about when one of the inmates took against me. So now I limp and I have scars and I can walk from one side of London to the other without anyone giving me a white feather because they all think I was wounded over there. You know what that's called, Alfie, don't you?'

Alfie shook his head.

'Irony,' replied Joe, smiling a little but not looking very happy as he did so. 'That's what they call irony. Read something other than *Robinson Crusoe* and you'll find that word pops up from time to time.'

'And the bruises on your face?' asked Alfie. 'The recent ones?'

'My own fault,' said Joe with a bitter smile. 'I shouldn't open my door at night. The drunks. They come after the pubs close.'

Alfie thought about this long and hard. He could hear himself breathing through his nose as he considered everything that Joe had told him, and through all this, Joe said nothing, just waited for him to speak.

'Don't you want to leave here?' said Alfie finally. 'People have been so horrible to you. Don't you want to go somewhere else?'

'Where would I go? This is my home.'

'Somewhere you could start again. You could get married, have children of your own.'

Joe smiled and shook his head. 'I don't think any woman would put up with me.'

'Why not? I read in the papers that all the girls are looking for husbands now. There's a death of young men in London now, that's what they say.'

'A dearth,' said Joe.

'And Helena Morris was sweet on you, everyone knows that. You could marry her.'

'I'd rather bore a hole to the centre of the earth with my tongue,' said Joe, tapping a hand on his knee and looking anxious. 'Some men were built for sweethearts, Alfie. Like your dad. I remember when he met your mum. I never saw a man so much in love! And she fell for him too. It was all so easy. So unfair. Some of us . . . well, we don't get that kind of luck.'

'Do you think my dad was wrong?' asked Alfie, uncertain what Joe was talking about but sure that it had something to do with the beliefs that had got him in so much trouble. 'To go to the war, I mean? Do you think he should have stayed at home and been a conchie like you?'

Joe Patience shook his head. 'I don't tell other people what to do,' he said. 'I don't tell them what they should think and what they shouldn't think. I just live my own life. Your dad is a brave man and he did what he thought was right. But I'm a brave man too. You might not believe that, Alfie, and those women in Trafalgar Square and Piccadilly Circus and strolling down Regent Street like they understand something about bravery might not believe it. But I am.'

'I want to bring him home,' said Alfie.

'Bring who home?'

'My dad.'

Joe frowned. 'But he's in the hospital.'

'He's not getting any better there. And it's a terrible place. It stinks and there's blood everywhere and all the patients are crying or going mad. I can't leave him there. If I bring him home, then Mum and me can help him get better. We'll fix him instead.'

Joe frowned and walked over to the window and looked out at the street. Mrs Milchin from number seven was walking by, and as she passed Joe's door she spat at it.

'You need to speak to your mum about this,' said Joe finally.

'No.'

'Why not?'

'After I discovered him I came straight home to tell mum,' said Alfie. 'I thought perhaps she really believed that he was on a secret mission for the Government. But that evening she'd already gone to the hospital for a night shift, and when she came back again, I was already asleep. And then, when she went to work the next day, I went to King's Cross to shine shoes—'

'To do what?'

'To shine shoes,' he repeated. 'I do that to help mum out. There might be a war going on but a lot of people want to have clean shoes. I'm doing my bit, amn't I? And I saw her board a train to Ipswich.

So she knows he's there anyway but she's decided to leave him there. She doesn't understand that it would be better to bring him home.'

Joe walked around the room a couple of times, agitated now. 'She's probably right, then, Alfie,' he said. 'The hospital's the best place for him. I know it's rotten in there, but we have to believe that the doctors know what they're doing. They'll look after him. They'll make him better.'

'But he barely recognized me!' shouted Alfie, standing up. 'He's not getting better. They won't fix him there. I can fix him. If he's back here where he belongs.'

'Alfie, why are you here?' asked Joe, throwing his hands up in the air. 'Why did you come to me with this?'

'Because Old Bill Hemperton said that you were your own man and my dad's your oldest friend, so I came here to ask you to help me.'

'To help you do what?'

'Break him out.'

Joe's eyes opened wide. 'Break him out?' he asked. 'You want to break your father out of hospital?'

'And bring him home. I can't do it alone. I thought you could help me.'

Joe shook his head. 'I can't do that, Alfie,' he said. 'You think you're helping him but you might only be making him worse.'

'No,' cried Alfie.

'You have to speak to your mum. Or your granny! Tell them what you know. Maybe you can all go there together. He might like a visit from the three people he loves the most in the—'

'No,' insisted Alfie. 'You have to help me. There's no one else who I can trust.'

'Well, I'm sorry,' said Joe, shaking his head. 'But I can't.'

Alfie turned his hands into fists and thumped the sofa in frustration. One of the pillows burst and all the stuffing flew out of it. He stared at the feathers as they floated in the air in front of him before grabbing one, a white one, and running across to press it against Joe's chest.

Joe stared at it blankly as he held it in his hands. 'Oh Alfie,' he said with a deep sigh filled with pain – more pain than Alfie thought he had ever heard in a man's voice before; and the moment he said his name, Alfie ran out into the corridor, threw open the front door and charged outside, running down Damley Road as fast as he could, wanting to put everyone from the street as far behind him as he possibly could.

11

PACK UP YOUR TROUBLES IN YOUR OLD KIT BAG

Alfie took an early train to the hospital, stepping into King's Cross Station just after ten o'clock in the morning. It was a Monday, and normally he would have been in school on a Monday – which was history day – but he had different plans for *this* Monday, the day he was planning on saving his father's life by breaking him out of hospital.

Carrying a duffel bag over his shoulder, he bought one return ticket from London to Ipswich and another single from Ipswich to London. (Georgie wouldn't be going back there, after all.) This time he found his platform without difficulty and settled into the corner of a carriage, talking to no one, and trying to lose himself in *Robinson Crusoe.*

Arriving close to where he and Marian had alighted the previous week, he looked around, wondering whether anyone else might be getting off here, and when it seemed as if he was the only one, he began to worry that the train wouldn't stop at all. But a few minutes later, to his relief, he felt the engines beginning to slow down and the train screeched to a halt as he hopped off, making his way down the narrow lane, towards the crossroads and along the path that led to the East Suffolk and Ipswich Hospital.

Outside the main gate, he waited for a few minutes, making sure that no one else was going to appear and want to know what he was doing there. He ran behind a tree to take care of some personal business and then, feeling that now was as good a time as any, sprinted up the driveway as fast as his legs could carry him. Through the front doors of the hospital, a dog appeared and growled at him, and Alfie stopped dead. He was a bit afraid of dogs; he had been ever since he'd been three and Jack Tamorin from number twenty's terrier had snapped at his hand while he was trying to feed it a bone. He watched, waiting to see what happened, but the dog seemed to lose interest in him and finally trotted back indoors and out of sight.

Who would bring a dog into a hospital? wondered Alfie. It didn't seem very hygienic.

A window opened behind him and he pressed himself against a wall as a young woman's head leaned out and looked down the drive. He was so close to her that he could have reached up and touched her, but she didn't glance down under the windowsill, just out towards the gates.

'There's no one there, Bessie,' she said, turning back. 'You're seeing things, you are. You've gone barmy. You need your Henry back, that's what you need.'

'Chance'd be a fine thing,' replied an unseen person from inside. 'He was somewhere outside Antwerp, last I heard. I'll be lucky if I see him again this side of Christmas.'

'It'll all be over by Christmas,' said the first girl, closing the window again, and whatever the response was to that, Alfie didn't hear. But he hoped it was suitably unimpressed.

He slipped round the corner of the building and down the path towards the gap in the hedge where the patients had been sitting outside in the sunshine the previous week, hoping that the young man with the lank dark hair who had grabbed his arm wouldn't be there, but this part of the garden was empty today; all the men must be indoors. The table that had held the newspapers and apples was still there, a blackbird perched on top of it, its head darting around as it scanned the table top for crumbs. Alfie stepped out into the clearing beyond and discovered two men sitting in their bath chairs, wrapped in heavy coats and with rugs across their knees. They both looked perfectly peaceful but were not speaking to each other. The second man had his back turned, like Georgie had the previous week, so Alfie couldn't make out his face.

'Hello there,' said the man closest to him, putting his book down on his lap and taking his spectacles off. 'And who might you be?'

Alfie looked at him and hesitated; he didn't want to get into any conversations with the men today but thought it best not to antagonize anyone in case they called for a doctor or nurse.

'Alfie Summerfield,' he said.

'I had a brother called Alfie,' said the man, smiling at him. 'His number got called at Ypres. Damned difficult word to say, Ypres, don't you think? It took me a long time to get it right.'

'Yes, sir,' said Alfie, stepping past him to make his way down to the man at the end.

'Don't go,' said the man, and something in his voice, something pleading, made Alfie stop and look at him. He wasn't really that old. No more than twenty-five. He didn't look like he'd suffered any injuries and seemed to have recently had a wash as he smelled of soap and his hair was fluffy. 'What are you doing here anyway? We don't get many boys your age around here. None at all, in fact.'

'I'm looking for my dad,' said Alfie.

'Is he a doctor?'

Alfie was about to say no, that he was a patient, but thought better of it. 'Yes,' he said. 'I thought he might be out here.'

'We only see the doctors indoors,' said the man. 'The nurses come and look after us here. Good thing too – they're a far prettier lot. But tell me, where were you?'

Alfie stared at him, uncertain what the question meant. 'Where was I?' he asked.

'Yes, where were you? France or Belgium?'

Alfie frowned. 'Neither,' he said.

The man leaned forward and frowned. 'You're not a conchie, are you?'

'No, sir.'

'Oh, all right, then,' he said with a sigh, leaning back. 'It hurts, doesn't it?'

'What does?' asked Alfie.

'Don't you hear it in your head? I do. Although it's peaceful in the garden. I ask them to bring me out here, regardless of the weather. Can't stand it inside. All that wailing and gnashing of teeth. It's positively biblical at times.'

As if on cue, there was a loud bang from the house, something like a door slamming as the wind rushed through a hallway. Alfie spun round in that direction, and when he looked back at the man, his eyes were closed and he seemed to be counting slowly in his head.

'Doctor Ridgewell tells me to do this,' he said after a moment, opening his eyes and attempting a smile. 'I'm quite all right, really. I'm being sent home on Monday. What day is today?'

'Monday,' said Alfie.

'Oh,' replied the man, considering this. 'Then they must have got it wrong. It's a difficult word to say, isn't it? *Ypres.* But then, that's the French for you. They don't like to make things easy. I knew a girl in Paris, you know. Fine little thing. Worked in a bistro off the Avenue de la Motte-Picquet. Thought about marrying her, but I know what my father would have said if I'd brought her home. Can't stand the continentals, you see. And he has money, so he assumes everyone wants some of it. Never cared for money much, myself. Easy to say, I suppose, when you have a lot of it.'

Alfie looked towards the man at the end of the garden and, as if he felt the boy's eyes on him, he turned round. It wasn't his dad.

'I have to go,' said Alfie.

'Off on your rounds, are you? You're young for a doctor, but I suppose we must all chip in at these times.'

Alfie nodded and stepped away. He hated it here. He hated this place and he hated these people. Being at this hospital was like stepping into the middle of a nightmare where nothing anyone said made any sense. The men were all confused, living partly in the present, partly in the past, and partly in some no man's land that they marched across, trying to dodge bullets and failing, flailing, falling. He was doing the right thing getting his dad away from here, he was sure of it. He picked up the duffel bag and made his way through the hedge and over towards the hospital.

He stood outside now, dreading the idea of going back inside, but there was no way around it. He had hoped that he would discover Georgie out in the grounds and that they could make their escape together, but this hadn't happened and he would have to go in search of him.

In one of those terrible wards.

He threw the duffel bag behind a potted plant and opened the door, poking his head inside. The coast was clear. There was a staircase halfway down the corridor and he looked up; it was at least three storeys high, with rooms on the perimeter of every floor. His heart sank, wondering how on earth he would ever find his dad in so large a place.

In front of him was the nurses' station where he had been discovered the last time, and he walked quickly towards it, pleased to see that there was no one there now. If the angry doctor found him again, he'd never believe his story about being the milkman's son. He looked around, stepped behind the desk, and as he did so he saw Dr Ridgewell, whose shoes he had shined twice now, emerging from one of the wards with another doctor, younger and nervous looking, and he slipped down behind the counter, hoping that they wouldn't come round to this side.

'. . . can go home early next week, I think,' Dr Ridgewell was saying. 'Book him in for some appointments with Davis in Harley Street. I've spoken to his secretary – she knows all about it. Once a week should be enough. It's encouraging though, isn't it? To see someone improve so much. It gives one hope for the others.'

'Have you heard anything from the War Office yet, Doctor?' said the younger man.

'About what?'

'Recognition.'

There was a silence for a few moments. 'Not yet, no. None of these bloody politicians wants to be the one to actually state the obvious, to make it clear to the public that this condition is real and that it's something we all have to deal with. We'll be dealing with it for years to come, I'm afraid. The problem is, the public still think of it as cowardice and no one in Parliament has the guts to tell them otherwise.'

'I thought . . .' said the young man. 'That is to say, I was wondering whether . . .'

'Oh, spit it out, Chartwell. I don't have all day.'

'Well, it's just that we've had some successes, haven't we? And some failures. Would it be helpful to invite some gentlemen of the press here? They could write about it. Put it about a bit with the general population. We might get a little more public support that way.'

Dr Ridgewell didn't say anything for a few moments, and when he did his tone suggested that he was astounded by the very idea. 'Gentlemen of the press?' he asked, slowly enunciating every word. 'Have you quite lost your reason, Chartwell? Invite the newspapers here? To the East Suffolk? Do you really think that's what our patients need – a load of gawking journalists interviewing them and taking pictures of them to sell papers?'

'I only meant that if we could tell the world what's going on here, then we might encourage them to speak to their local Members of Parliament. We could show them people like Boyars, since he's going home practically mended. We could tell them about the good work we're doing.'

'And what about those who aren't getting any better, Chartwell – have you thought about them? Levinson on the first floor? Hobbs in the ward next to him? Summerfield on the second? Should we wheel them out too and make a spectacle of them to the world and its mother? Am I to become P. T. Barnum, and these unfortunate men my circus freaks?'

Alfie's ears pricked up when he heard his own surname being mentioned. *Summerfield on the second.*

'I'm sorry, Doctor,' said the young man, a note of contrition in his tone now. 'It was a bad idea.'

'It would have to be a considerably better idea, Chartwell, to qualify as a bad idea. It would have many degrees of stupidity to get through before it could aspire to such an elevated term. No, let's just get on with what we do best – the practice of medicine – and leave the outside world to think what they will think. Now, I can't stand around here all day chinwagging. I have patients to see and I'm sure that you do too.'

And to Alfie's relief, they started to walk away and never noticed him hiding there.

He jumped out from behind the counter and began climbing the stone stairs, reaching the landing of the first floor and continuing up to the second. At least he knew his father's floor now. There was the murmur of low voices here – patients in their rooms, nurses tending to them – and he tiptoed quietly along, looking into the first ward, trying to stay quiet so that no one would notice him.

It was difficult to identify his father, though, for so many of the men were either curled up in their beds with the blankets pulled up to their faces or sitting in chairs with their backs to him, staring out of the window. His heart sank, and he didn't know what to do – but that was when he saw him, in a ward with the words ST MARGARET'S written above the door, seated by the window, shuffling a pack of cards, pulling different ones out at random and staring at them for a few moments before putting them back in.

Alfie stepped inside and looked around. There were three other men in the ward. The first was lying in the bed to Alfie's left and was fast asleep, a blanket pulled up to his chin while his hands gripped it like a small child. Opposite him was another man, sitting up and reading a book. He put it down when he saw Alfie and started grinning. He didn't have any teeth. Alfie raised a hand and held it in the air for a moment, and the man shook his head and looked away. In the third bed was a very young man – he didn't look more than about eighteen – lying down with his hands clenched into fists, which he held at the sides of his head. Every few seconds his eyes would close tightly and he would emit a strange sound, like a gasp of horror; then the moment would pass and his fists would unclench again before it all began once more. And finally, there, by the window, was Georgie Summerfield.

'Dad,' said Alfie, reaching him and kneeling down before him. 'Dad, it's me. Alfie.'

Georgie stared at him, and the signs of recognition appeared on his face. He already seemed better than he had last week. 'Alfie,' he said. 'It's never you.'

'It is,' said Alfie. 'I told you I'd come back.'

'When did you tell me, Alfie? I'm not dreaming this, am I? Come here to me, son.'

Alfie moved forward and Georgie put both hands out to touch Alfie's face. His fingers moved across his cheeks and chin, the way a blind man's might if he wanted to find out something about you. 'It is you, isn't it?' he said, in a quiet voice, amazement mixed with emotion. 'But you've grown so big. You're not five any more, are you?'

'I'm nine,' said Alfie, confused, for his father had seen him only a few days earlier but seemed to have completely forgotten about it. He glanced at the bedside locker, where three different-coloured pills were laid out on a tin plate beside a glass of water, and he wondered how much medicine they were giving Georgie every day and whether it was making him forget things.

'Nine,' said his dad, shaking his head in wonder. 'You're not here now too, are you?' he asked suddenly, an expression of horror crossing his face before he shook his head. 'No, of course you're not. I'm not thinking straight, you're just a boy. You couldn't be. But then what are you doing here? Who let you in?'

'I've come for you, Dad,' said Alfie.

'For me?'

'To take you home.'

Georgie swallowed and shook his head. 'I can't go home,' he said. 'I'm not well, Alfie.'

'You're not well because this place is making you not well. But if you come home with me I'll make you better. I promise! You need to get back on the milk float. Mr Asquith is still there, you know. He misses you something rotten.'

'Who?'

'Mr Asquith,' repeated Alfie. 'You know! Mr Asquith!'

'Oh yes,' said Georgie, shaking his head slowly as if he had no idea what Alfie was talking about.

'I can come to work with you,' said Alfie. 'You said I could when I was older.'

'Five is too young for the floats. Your mother would have my guts for garters.'

'But I'm *nine* now, Dad! Nine!'

A sound came from the boy in the bed opposite and Alfie looked across at him. His eyes were open but they didn't seem to be focused on anything.

'He's barely said anything sensible in a week, poor blighter,' said Georgie, shaking his head. 'His mind's done for.'

'Dad, you have to come with me,' said Alfie, tugging at his father's hand. 'We can leave, both of us. There's a train. I've got two tickets. I'll take you home. You'll get better if you just come home.'

'All right, Alfie,' said Georgie, shrugging his shoulders as if he didn't have any choice in the matter. 'Doctor Ridgewell's said it's all right, did he?'

Alfie hesitated but then nodded quickly. 'Yes,' he replied. 'He says you're better and all you need is to go home to your family. He told me to come and get you.'

'He never said anything about it to me. Ow,' he cried suddenly, grimacing and putting a hand to his temple. 'Pills, pills,' he grunted, pointing at the dish beside the bed, and Alfie ran over to get them and the glass of water. Georgie swallowed each one quickly and sat back in his chair, breathing heavily as if this had already exhausted him. 'It's the headaches,' he said quietly. 'I get them every so often. Rotten things, they are. Pain like you wouldn't believe. They make me sick. I need my pills, Alfie. They give me them every three hours. Don't let's go without them.'

'It's fine, Dad,' said Alfie, who knew there was a medicine cabinet in the bathroom at home next to the bandages, a gloopy green bottle for when he had a cough, and a couple of bottles of pills – he didn't know what for. 'We've lots of pills at home. You can have some of those.'

'Oh, all right, then, Alfie,' said Georgie, shrugging his shoulders again, and it was only now that Alfie realized that his dad wasn't behaving like his dad any more. It was as if they'd swapped roles and Georgie simply believed whatever Alfie told him; as if he was the adult and Georgie the child. This idea made Alfie feel very uncomfortable and even a little frightened. His dad was supposed to take care of him, not the other way around.

'Come on, then,' he said, pulling his father up again and leading the way out of the ward. 'We need to go downstairs quietly.'

'Bye, lads!' said Georgie cheerfully, waving at the men in the beds, but his voice was too loud and Alfie shushed him. They made their way to the ground floor without anyone noticing them, and out into the courtyard, where Alfie retrieved his duffel bag; he opened it up and pulled out the trousers, shirt and jacket that he'd taken from his dad's wardrobe that morning.

'Put these on,' said Alfie. 'That way no one will grow suspicious on the train.'

'All right, Alfie,' said Georgie, obediently putting the clothes on over his pyjamas and then slipping on the shoes that Alfie handed him. 'You are sure about this, though, aren't you? Doctor Ridgewell says it's fine?'

'He told me to come and get you,' said Alfie. 'Come on, Dad, let's go.'

As they turned the corner, Alfie saw a man marching towards them wearing a full dress uniform and he felt his heart jump in his chest. The man was staring at the two of them and picking up his pace as he got closer.

'Don't say anything, Dad,' whispered Alfie. 'Leave this to me, all right?'

'All right, Alfie,' said Georgie.

'You, boy,' said the man, stopping now before

them. He had very red cheeks and a snow-white moustache and was carrying something resembling a cane in his hands. 'Where am I?'

'The East Suffolk and Ipswich Hospital,' said Alfie.

'Yes, I know that,' said the man irritably. 'I'm not completely stupid, you know. I'm looking for the entrance to B wing. There's a bloody great dog down there at the main doors, and every time I try to go in he growls at me. I would have shot him but I left my gun at GHQ.'

Alfie stared at him in horror. For a moment he wondered whether this was just another one of the patients, but the man's uniform said otherwise.

'Who are you anyway?' asked the man. 'What's a boy doing here? And who's this fellow?'

'Georgie Summerfield,' said Georgie, smiling as if the whole thing was a terrific joke. 'I had a dog myself when I was a boy. A little King Charles. Melancholy little fellow. But full of love.'

'Fascinating,' said the man. 'Work here, do you, Georgie?'

'*Doctor* Summerfield,' said Alfie quickly.

'Oh,' said the man, looking him up and down and backing off a little. 'You're in charge around here, are you?'

'Not me, sir, no,' said Georgie.

'Doctor Summerfield is just leaving for the day,' said Alfie.

'At this time?' asked the man, checking his watch. 'Bit early to down tools, isn't it?'

'He was on the night shift,' said Alfie.

'And what are you, the ventriloquist's dummy? Can't Doctor Summerfield speak for himself? Who are you anyway?'

'His father is a patient here,' said Georgie, standing up straight now and speaking in a clear voice.

'And how's he doing?'

'Not well. He came to see him, but we can't have boys here. I'm making sure he gets back to the station on my way out.'

'Hmm,' said the man. 'Very well. Give him a clip around the ear, did you?'

'No, sir,' said Georgie.

'I would have. Can't abide boys, me. Or girls. Any children really. Either gender. I don't discriminate. Hate them both equally. Well, look . . . B wing – help me out, will you?'

'Go through this door,' said Alfie, 'then walk down the corridor, take the first left and you'll come to a staircase, go up one flight and turn right until you reach St Hilda's Ward, then go through the door that says *No Entry*, and the long corridor there will lead you to B wing.'

'Thank you,' said the man, nodding cheerfully now. 'Think I got all that.'

'You're welcome,' said Alfie, who had made

every word of that last speech up. But he simply wanted the man to leave and hopefully to get lost in the corridors of the East Suffolk.

'You did brilliant, Dad,' said Alfie when the man was gone, but Georgie had relapsed into his former absent state now and it took him a long time to turn his head.

'What was that, Alfie?'

'You were just like your old self. He didn't suspect a thing.'

Georgie said nothing, simply frowned and then closed his eyes as he let a low groan emerge from his mouth and pressed his hands to his temples.

'Dad,' said Alfie. 'Dad, are you all right?'

'Fine, son,' said Georgie quietly. 'Can we go back inside now? I think I should get back to my bed.'

'No! I'm taking you home, remember?'

'Oh yes,' he replied. 'All right, then. If that's what you think is best.'

Halfway down the drive, Alfie saw three nurses coming up it, and he pushed his father behind a group of trees.

'What's going on?' asked Georgie, looking around as if he'd just woken up.

'Ssh!' said Alfie. 'Don't make a sound.'

'Sergeant Clayton on the prowl, is he?'

'Dad! Ssh!' insisted Alfie, watching the nurses as they passed.

'I was only asking.'

'Dad!' Alfie felt himself breaking out into a sweat. All it would take was for one of the nurses to turn her head and she would surely see them hiding in the greenery. He held his breath and only exhaled again after they had passed by. 'Right,' he said. 'Come on, we need to get out of here as fast as we can.'

He broke into a run, and Georgie watched in confusion for a moment before running after him. When they were clear of the hospital gates, they stopped and caught their breath. 'The train station's down here,' said Alfie. 'Just follow me.'

'Alfie,' said Georgie as they sat down on the grass a few minutes later, waiting for the train to arrive. 'You did remember my pills, didn't you?'

'I told you,' said Alfie. 'There's plenty of pills at home. You can have some of those. But you won't need them, I promise. Once you're back home in Damley Road, you'll be right as rain.'

'All right, Alfie,' said Georgie, nodding his head, satisfied.

'All right, Dad,' said Alfie.

12

I WANT TO GO HOME

Georgie remained very quiet on the train back to London. He sat in the corner of the carriage, staring out at the passing scenery, his arms wrapped around his chest as if he was trying to stop himself from rocking back and forth. Whenever it stopped at a station – or *near* a station – to let passengers on or off, he closed his eyes. When the conductor blew his whistle, and at one particularly busy stop, when the doors were being slammed all the way down the train, Alfie was sure he could hear a low groan emerging from his mouth. At these moments he tried to talk to him, but his dad would only reply with single word answers: *yes*; *no*; *Clayton*; *tomorrow*; *pills*; *sometimes*; *help*.

At Manningtree a young Tommy climbed aboard and sat in the carriage with them, lighting up a cigarette and looking from one to the other with an arrogant, cheeky smile on his face. His uniform was clean and freshly pressed; it looked as if he was wearing it for the first time. Georgie looked him up and down for a moment, a distressed expression on his face, but when the soldier caught his eye he turned away.

'What you looking at?' he asked. 'Never seen a soldier before?'

Georgie said nothing, and Alfie tried to concentrate on *Robinson Crusoe* so he wouldn't think of talking to him.

'Cat got your tongue? I said, *Never seen a soldier before?*'

'Seen a few,' muttered Georgie, staring out of the window.

'What's that you're reading?' asked the soldier, flipping the book out of Alfie's hands in a deft move and spinning it round to read the cover. '*Robinson Crusoe.* My old dad has a copy of this at home. Looks boring.'

'It's the best book ever written,' said Alfie.

'Ha,' said the soldier, shaking his head. 'As if you would know. Who's the barrel of laughs in the window seat?' he asked, nodding in Georgie's direction.

'My dad,' said Alfie.

'Got a screw loose, has he? Hey, you! You got a screw loose, do you?'

Georgie turned round and stared at him for a moment, cocking his head to the side as if he was trying to understand exactly what was going on, before turning to look out of the window again.

'Here, what do you think?' continued the young Tommy, pointing at his uniform. 'Looks pretty smart, doesn't it? It's my first day. On my way to London to meet my new pals, then on to Aldershot to start training. I've been waiting for this day for four years. They said it would be over by Christmas, didn't they? Thank Christ they were wrong about that. Here, why aren't you fighting, mate?' he asked, shouting over at Georgie, who immediately stood up and walked out of the carriage, shutting the door behind him furiously. 'Feather man, is he?' he asked, laughing, and Alfie felt his hands twist into fists, wishing he could shut this fool up. 'They're everywhere, they are. Takes a real man to win a war. I'll sort out Fritz, never you mind about that. Me and my new pals.'

Alfie stood up and left the carriage without a word, making his way through the train, and finally discovered his father sitting alone, his head buried in his hands.

'Dad?' he said, sitting down next to him. He wanted desperately to put his arm around him but he didn't know how; it felt too awkward. 'Dad, are you all right?'

'I'm fine, Alfie,' replied Georgie in a low voice. 'I'm just tired, that's all. You don't have any of those pills on you, do you?'

'No, sorry.'

'All right, then.'

They didn't say anything else all the way back to King's Cross, and when they arrived, Georgie seemed unwilling to get off the train, the sound of the screeching engines and the whistles of the conductors making him tremble visibly. When Alfie finally coaxed him out onto the platform, he seemed even less happy to be led back in the direction of Damley Road. When they reached the top of the street, Alfie peeped round the corner first, hoping that no one would be in sight, but there was Mrs Scutworth from number fifteen and Mrs Candlemas from number thirteen standing side by side, washing their windows.

'We'll just wait until they're finished,' said Alfie, and Georgie nodded.

They stood and waited and the minutes ticked by. Every time Alfie looked at his dad, he wanted to say something to him, but Georgie's forehead was wrinkled and he seemed to be crouched over a little, his fists clenched, his body rocking back and forth, and Alfie couldn't think of anything to say that wouldn't make things worse.

'Come on, Dad,' he said finally, when the two women had gone back inside their houses, and he found himself taking his father by the hand and leading him down the street to his front door, just as Georgie had done with him when he was a little boy. He put his key in the lock, twisted it quickly, and let them both inside.

Georgie looked around; he seemed a little unsteady on his feet. Nothing much had changed in the four years since he'd last been here, but perhaps the memory of number twelve was too much for him, for the moment he stepped inside the front parlour he fell into the broken armchair in front of the fireplace and buried his face in his hands.

'. . . when they saw it was us, they were different, weren't they?' he mumbled to himself. 'I can't be on stretcher-bearer duty again – three nights in a row is too much for any man, it's torture . . . *Stay where you are and then leave* – that's what he told me. Makes no sense, does it? Where's Unsworth? Where's he got himself now?'

'Dad!' said Alfie, kneeling down beside him. 'Dad, what's wrong? I don't understand what you mean.'

Georgie looked up and shook his head, and for a moment he seemed more like his old self. 'What's that, son?' he asked in a cheerful voice. 'Oh, don't mind me, I was away with the fairies, that's all. Ask your mum to make us a nice cup of tea, there's a good lad. I need an early night if I'm to be up in the morning.'

Alfie nodded and stepped into the kitchen, putting the water on the range to boil. He looked in the tea caddy: it was a quarter full, so he put a spoonful in the teapot, filled it with the hot water and left it to stew for a few minutes while he took some bread and cheese from the larder. When the tea was brewed, he put everything on a tray and brought it into the parlour. Georgie was standing by the fireplace, holding a portrait of the three of them – himself, Margie and Alfie – taken only a few weeks before the war began.

'Nice-looking family,' said Georgie as if he didn't recognize any of them.

'Dad, that's us,' said Alfie, handing the tea across. 'Here, drink this. You'll feel better, I promise.'

Georgie nodded and sat down with the cup, taking a careful sip. 'You forgot the sugar,' he said. 'Never mind, we're probably out. Think on, if we were back in London, my Margie would never forget the sugar.'

Alfie stared at him. 'Dad, this *is*—'

There was a *rat-a-tat-tat* on the front door and Alfie jumped. Only one person ever knocked on the door like that. 'Stay in here,' he said, turning to his father. 'Don't move, all right?'

'Yes, sir!' said Georgie, saluting as he sat back in the chair.

Alfie stepped outside into the hallway and opened the front door only a little, looking out into the street but keeping his right foot positioned so no one could just walk in.

'All right, Alfie?'

'All right, Old Bill,' he said, smiling at his next-door neighbour, who was peering over his shoulder into the corridor. Behind him, Alfie could see Mr Asquith standing in the middle of the road with Henry Lyons sitting on the bench-seat behind, the milk float filled with empty churns. He was doing everything he could to get the horse to trot on, but Mr Asquith was staring intently at number twelve and would not move under any circumstances.

'Everything all right in there?' asked Old Bill.

'Yes. Mum's at work, though, if you were looking for her.'

'No, it's not that,' he said. 'Alfie, I might be going mad, but I was coming into my front room a few minutes ago and glanced outside, and I could have sworn that I saw a familiar face passing by my window.'

Alfie swallowed and hoped that his expression wouldn't give him away. He tried to look as if he didn't understand.

'A familiar face?' he asked. 'Whose?'

'You all alone in there, Alfie?' asked Old Bill.

'*Come on, old chap!*' cried Henry Lyons at the top of his voice.

'I told you: Mum's at work.'

Old Bill scratched his beard and seemed uncertain whether or not he should ask more questions. 'I thought I saw . . . Well, look, I know this sounds crazy, but I thought I saw your dad walking down Damley Road. Large as life and twice as ugly.' He turned round and stared at Mr Asquith. 'What the flamin' 'ell is wrong with that horse?'

'My dad?' asked Alfie, laughing out loud, and even to him it sounded fake.

'Yes, your dad. You know – tall bloke. Went away to the war. Your dad, Alfie.'

'My dad's on a secret mission,' said Alfie.

'Then my eyes must have been playing tricks on me.'

'I suppose so.'

'I must have been dreaming.'

'There's no one else here.'

'Can I come in, Alfie?' asked Old Bill.

'I've got to go to school.'

Old Bill glanced at his watch. 'At this time?' he said.

'I mean the shops. I told Mum I'd get something in for our tea.'

There was a long pause and they stared at each other, man and boy, waiting for each other to crack. Finally, with a great neighing sound, Mr Asquith lunged forward down the street, clip-clopping along, turning his head back once or twice to look at Alfie reproachfully.

'Right you are,' said Old Bill finally, sighing

deeply. 'Well, I suppose I'll see you later on. Goodbye, Alfie.'

'Goodbye, Old Bill.'

He closed the door and stood with his back to it for a moment, shaking his head. That had been close. When he went back into the parlour, Georgie's cup was lying on the floor, the tea seeping into the carpet at his feet. He looked up at Alfie like a little child who has been discovered doing something he shouldn't.

'I dropped it,' he said.

'It doesn't matter,' said Alfie. 'It'll dry out.'

'No, I better clean it up,' he said, reaching for one of the cushions from the sofa and moving to press it down on the damp spot.

'No, don't do that,' said Alfie, grabbing the cushion away from him. His mum would go mad if he got tea on that. 'It doesn't matter. Just leave it.'

'Yes, sir, Sarge,' said Georgie, sitting back again.

'I'm not a sarge!' cried Alfie in frustration. 'I'm Alfie!'

'Of course you are, son,' said Georgie with a shrug. 'I know my own son, don't I?'

Alfie glanced over at the clock on the sideboard. It was the middle of the afternoon now and he realized that he had never really thought about what he would do once he'd brought his father home again; he had just wanted to get him out of that terrible hospital, with its blood and its stench and the constant groaning of damaged men in the air. But now he realized that maybe being cooped up inside this small house wasn't the best thing for Georgie right now, and an idea struck him. He ran up to his bedroom, opened his wardrobe, took the shoeshine box from its storage place and came back downstairs. 'We're going out,' he said, looking at his father.

'Out? Where to? I was just getting comfortable.'

'I have to go to work.'

Georgie frowned. 'Work? The dairy won't be open now. Not for us anyway.'

'I don't work at the dairy,' said Alfie. 'I work at King's Cross.'

'Train driver, are you? They're a posh old lot, them train drivers.'

'I'm a shoeshine boy,' said Alfie in frustration.

'Well, that's a good honest way to make a living.' His dad gazed around and suddenly looked as if he didn't recognize where he was. 'I need to get out of here,' he said in a tone of sudden terror.

'Good, because that's what we're doing. Come on.'

They left the house, and this time Alfie walked Georgie the long way round, ushering his father ahead of him, so that they wouldn't pass Old Bill Hemperton's front window. At the end of the street he turned round for a moment and saw Joe Patience standing in his doorway smoking a cigarette and watching him. How long had he been standing there? Had he seen Georgie? Their eyes met for a moment, but Joe gave nothing away, just continued to smoke, and Alfie turned the corner, where his father was waiting for him, staring up at the sky.

'It's a big world, isn't it?' said Georgie. 'Do you think they all hate each other on other planets too?'

'This is my spot,' said Alfie when he reached his usual place at King's Cross, equidistant between the platforms, the ticket counter and the teashop. 'And that's the chair I let the customers sit in. Do you want to sit on it?'

Georgie shrugged, so Alfie pulled it over and his dad stared at it for a few moments before sitting down. Alfie took his brushes, dusters and cloths out of the shoeshine box and fitted the footrest on top of it as his father watched, saying nothing.

'I took this from Mr Janáček's house,' he explained. 'After he and Kalena got taken away. The soldiers thought they were Germans but they weren't, they were from Prague. I know I shouldn't have, but I don't think Mr Janáček would have minded. You're not angry with me, are you, Dad?' he asked.

Georgie shook his head. He stared at the boy and smiled. Alfie didn't understand why his dad's mood kept changing the way it did. 'No, son, I'm not angry with you,' he said. 'Mr Janáček would be happy to know that it was being put to good use.'

'I come here four days a week. I give most of the money I make to Mum. She's been working as a Queen's Nurse, you know. And taking in washing. And doing a bit of sewing for some posh piece. But I keep a little bit for myself for a rainy day. That's how I paid for the train tickets.'

Georgie nodded and reached into the pocket of his jacket. There was nothing there, so he reached into the other one. Nothing there either. Alfie knew what he was looking for. All the men who sat down here did that. They reached for their pipe or a cigarette. Everyone liked a smoke when they were getting their shoes shined. Even the Prime Minister.

'Would you like me to shine your shoes for you, Dad?' asked Alfie, looking down at his father's feet, and Georgie nodded and put his left foot on the footrest as Alfie got to work. There was a lot of dust on them from all the time they'd spent in the upstairs wardrobe. He had to give them a good dusting before he could start with the polish.

'Can you come home, Dad?' said Alfie quietly, not looking up as his fingers moved across the shoe.

'This *is* home, isn't it? London? Or have I gone mad?'

'I mean, *home* home,' said Alfie. 'For good. Back to Damley Road. Back to the milk float and Mr Asquith. Back to the way things used to be.'

A drop of water fell on the tip of his father's left shoe, and Alfie frowned as he wiped it off. The roof must be leaking. He looked around at the crowds making their way through King's Cross, and for a moment he thought he saw a familiar face over by the tobacconist's, watching him. A beaten face. Scars and burns. He blinked and tried to focus his eyes, but the people walking to and fro blocked his view, and when they parted, there was no one there.

'I hate the war,' said Alfie with a sigh.

'Everyone does,' said Georgie. 'It's rotten to the core.'

'They said it would be over by Christmas, but it wasn't.'

'Even when it ends, there'll be another one along soon enough. They're like buses, aren't they? You miss one, you'll catch the next one. You need to get away from here, Alfie, you hear me? Don't let them take you. We need thirty years of peace if you aren't to be called up.'

Another drop of water fell on the shoe, and Alfie lifted his head. The roof wasn't leaking; his dad was crying. He'd never seen him cry before and it frightened him. 'Dad,' he said. 'What's wrong?'

'Nothing, son, nothing,' he replied, wiping his face with his handkerchief. 'Don't mind me. Just make sure you get those shoes sparkling, all right? I might take your mum to a dance later. What time does she get home from work?'

Alfie shrugged. 'She might have a night shift,' he said. 'But if she does, she'll probably cancel it since you're back home. Although sometimes when she gets home she—'

A terrible noise came from behind them – the sound of twenty train carriage doors being slammed shut one after another. Alfie looked up – he'd heard this sound dozens of times a day ever since he'd started working here and hated it; it was like gunfire, rapid reports one after another, and seemed to go on for ever – but when he looked at his father, Georgie was holding his hands over his ears, crouched over, his head down.

'Dad,' said Alfie, sitting up. 'Dad, what's wrong?'

A horrible cry was coming from his father, a mixture of groaning and weeping, and Alfie looked over towards the train; there were still about ten more doors to go.

Bang! Bang! Bang! Bang!

'Dad!'

'Alfie, help me,' he pleaded. 'Stop them . . .'

Bang! Bang! Bang!

'Alfie, get down! Keep your head covered.'

Bang!

'On the count of three, we go over the top, all right? Three!'

Bang!

'Two!'

Bang!

'One!'

He took his hands away from his face and leaped from the chair, but Alfie was too quick for him and grabbed him around the waist, stopping him from running away.

'Dad, it's all right, it's me, it's Alfie. It was just the train doors slamming, that's all.'

Georgie looked across the platform, and slowly, very slowly, started to nod, understanding now. His face was pale. There was perspiration trailing its way down his forehead. His legs seemed to give way under him and he sat back on the seat.

'My pills, Alfie,' he said. 'I need my pills. My head is pounding.'

Alfie's stomach turned in anger at himself. He'd forgotten the pills from the medicine cabinet. He'd have to wait until he got home.

'I don't have them,' he said. 'I'm sorry, Dad, I left them at home. We can go back and get them if you like.'

'Can't do that,' groaned Georgie, reaching into his pockets again. 'A smoke at least. Dempster in the next foxhole has a pack. Tell him I'll give him two on Tuesday if he gives me one now. That's a good deal, isn't it?'

Alfie nodded. He reached for his cap on the ground and took out the few pennies that he always left there to encourage customers. The tobacconist's was at the very end, by platform six. 'I'll get you some,' he said.

'Dempster,' insisted Georgie.

'Yes, I'll ask him. One now, two for him on Tuesday. Got it.' He stared at his dad for a moment, uncertain about leaving him there alone, but it would be more trouble to get him to stand up and come over to the end of the concourse. If he ran over alone he could be back in less than two minutes.

'Stay where you are,' Alfie said in a determined voice. 'Do you hear me, Dad? Stay where you are.'

'And then leave,' muttered Georgie – this phrase again that he kept repeating over and over.

'What *is* that?' asked Alfie, kneeling down before him for a moment. 'What does that mean?'

'The sergeant,' said Georgie, staring at the ground. 'He said it to us before we went over the top every night. He made us line up on the ladders. A row of men with their heads almost level with the ground. The next set of men a few steps below, ready to follow. The next set at the base of the trench, ready to put their feet on the ladder. We were to wait until each row went over the top and then it was our turn. We weren't to move until the men in front of us had disappeared into the smoke and the gunfire. *Stay where you are and then leave,* that's what he told us. *Stay where you are and then leave.* Every night. Every night, Alfie.'

He pressed his hands to his temples again and gave a low cry of pain, like an animal caught in a trap, and Alfie turned on his heel, running towards the tobacconist's shop. This would take away the pain, he was sure it would. There was someone in front of him, taking for ever to count out his coins, and he looked back to make sure that his father was still in the seat, but the early evening crowds had started to gather and he couldn't see through them.

'Ten cigarettes,' said Alfie, throwing his coins on the counter when it was finally his turn.

'What kind?' asked the man behind the counter.

'Any kind! It doesn't matter. The cheapest ones.'

The man nodded and reached behind him, opening a drawer and taking an empty box from one of the shelves and counting them out. A train conductor's whistle blew, a shrill sound, before he shouted that the train to Liverpool was about to depart from platform three, the platform closest to Alfie's shoeshine stand.

'Quickly, please!' cried Alfie, looking round, and there he was again – a figure breaking through the crowd. Someone Alfie knew, but gone too quickly for him to recognize. He looked around; confusion everywhere. Noise. Movement.

'More haste, less speed,' said the tobacconist. 'I don't want to count out the wrong number, do I?'

People were running towards the train now, and there was the sound of the steam engine whistling through its funnel. He could see the conductor heading over, a long row of open doors before him.

'Ten cigarettes,' said the tobacconist. 'That'll be thru'pence please.'

Bang!

The first of the doors on the Liverpool train being slammed.

Bang! Bang! Bang!

'You're a farthing short,' said the man, and Alfie let out a cry of despair as he reached into his pocket and found a single farthing at the bottom of it. 'Here,' he said, grabbing the packet and throwing the coin across the counter.

Bang! Bang! Bang! Bang! Bang!

He ran through the crowd, almost tumbling over as he tried to force his way between them to return to his father.

'All aboard!'

Bang! Bang! Bang!

'Watch where you're going, boy!'

'Sorry.'

Bang! Bang! Bang! Bang!

Finally he broke through. He was back in his

usual spot and breathed a sigh of relief. He bent over, a stitch in his side, relieved to see that the chair in front of the shoeshine box was still occupied. When he stood up straight again, he reached out and handed the packet across.

'Cigarettes?' asked Mr Podgett, the man from the bank. 'Thank you, but I'm a pipe man. Is this a new service, then? A shoeshine and a free cigarette? Very enterprising of you, young man, but I'm not sure it's a very good idea. It'll eat into your profits.'

Alfie stared at him, his eyes opening wide as he turned, staring around the station. He couldn't see his father anywhere. He was gone.

He'd stayed where he was.

And then left.

13

THERE'S A LONG, LONG TRAIL A-WINDING

Alfie ran through the front door of number twelve and collapsed on the bottom stair with his head in his hands. He thought about everything that had happened that day and couldn't believe how stupid he'd been. He should never have taken Georgie out of the hospital – of course he shouldn't! How could he have been so stupid? But he had only ever wanted to help his dad, to bring him home to his family. And now he had lost him. What would he do if he was never found again?

He heard voices in the parlour and looked up in hope. Perhaps Georgie had found his way back again? He jumped up and ran inside to find Margie sitting on the broken armchair in front of the fireplace talking to someone on the sofa. He spun round, hoping that he would see his father sitting there – but no, it was Granny Summerfield.

'Alfie,' she said. 'What's the matter with you?

You have a guilty expression and I can't bear a boy with a guilty expression.'

He looked at his mother, who narrowed her eyes at him suspiciously. 'You do look pale,' said Margie. 'And your eyes are red. Have you been crying?'

Alfie shook his head. As it happened, he *hadn't* been crying, but he had been sitting with his head in his hands so that might have accounted for the redness.

'No,' he said.

'Where have you been, Alfie?' asked Granny Summerfield, leaning forward and taking off her spectacles. 'You have the look of a boy who's been up to no good.'

'I haven't done anything!' he shouted, raising his voice in a way that he had never done in front of his grandmother before.

'Alfie!' said Margie.

'What?' he asked, staring at her before throwing his arms up in the air. 'I'm going to my room,' he added, running into the hallway, charging upstairs and into his bedroom, where he slammed the door shut behind him and flung himself on the bed as he thought through the events of the last couple of hours.

Georgie had gone missing when he'd been at the tobacconist's stall and Alfie guessed that it was the sound of all the train doors slamming that had disturbed him. He had already reacted badly to them. And then there had been the way he talked – so strangely, and with sentences that didn't fit together correctly. He remembered what Dr Ridgewell had said to him about shell shock: how some of the soldiers who came back from the Front looked as if there was nothing wrong with them physically but inside, in their heads, they were very ill. That was how so many of the men at the East Suffolk had seemed to him. Even the amputees and the burns victims and the men with their arms in slings or their legs in harnesses had stared into the distance or rocked back and forth or sat crying, apparently hurting more than anyone he had ever seen, even more than he had hurt the day Charlie Slipton from number twenty-one threw a stone at him in the street for no reason whatsoever.

He must have run out of the station, Alfie reasoned, when the train doors were slamming. He must have panicked. But where would he go? He might have boarded a train, gone anywhere, and at some point in the journey the conductor would ask for his ticket, he wouldn't have one, and he'd be thrown off at the next stop. And what would happen then? A man wearing only pyjamas under an old pair of trousers and a jacket. How would he ever find his way home again?

There was a *rat-a-tat-tat* on the front door and

Alfie jumped up. He heard the parlour door opening and Margie marching out into the hall as voices drifted up the stairs, slipped under the door-way and into his room. He stepped out onto the landing and listened.

'Bill,' said Margie.

'Sorry to disturb you, Margie, old girl,' said Old Bill Hemperton. 'This is probably something and nothing but I thought I should come and tell you about it.'

'Come into the parlour,' she said. 'Granny Summerfield is here too.'

And with that they disappeared into the front room and closed the door behind them and Alfie couldn't hear them any more. He stood there, biting his lip, uncertain whether or not he should go downstairs. There was only one thing that Old Bill could have been calling in to say; the same thing he'd called over for earlier.

For a moment Alfie wondered whether he should pack a bag with some clothes, his shoeshine box, the money he had left in his sock drawer and his copy of *Robinson Crusoe* and make a run for it. He could get back to King's Cross and take a train somewhere, anywhere, start a new life. What did he need apart from his shoeshine box, after all? *That's a good honest way to make a living*, as Georgie had said.

'*Alfie!*'

The door in the parlour opened and Margie roared up the stairs to him. He stepped quickly back into his bedroom and closed the door.

'*Alfie!*' she shouted again. '*Come down these stairs.*'

There was nothing he could do. He opened his door and came down slowly, walking into the parlour where Margie was sitting, looking pale with worry. Old Bill looked remorseful and Granny Summerfield was crying into her handkerchief and saying, 'What's next? What's next for us now?'

'Sorry about this, sport,' said Old Bill, shrugging his shoulders. 'But a man's gotta do what a man's gotta do and all that rot. No hard feelings?'

Alfie said nothing; simply looked at his mother and waited for her to speak.

'Tell me Bill is wrong,' she said finally, her voice shaking a little.

'About what?'

'Alfie, I'm going to ask you this only once. Who did you bring back to this house this afternoon?'

Alfie thought about it and hesitated. '*This* afternoon?' he asked, as if there were any number of people he brought here generally but he couldn't be quite certain who had come here today.

'Alfie!'

'No one,' he said quickly. 'There wasn't anyone here. Just me.'

'Bill says different.'

'Bill's a hundred years old. He's half mad.'

'Strike me!' said Old Bill, shaking his head and laughing.

'Alfie, has your father been here? Tell me the truth.'

Alfie swallowed hard and felt he was on the verge of tears. He mumbled something under his breath, and Margie stepped forward so quickly that he took a step back in fright.

'What did you say?' she asked, raising her voice.

'*You said he was on a secret mission for the Government!*' roared Alfie. 'That's what you told me. But he wasn't. He was in hospital. And you didn't let me go and see him.'

'Oh Alfie,' said Margie quietly, sinking into the broken armchair in front of the fireplace. 'What have you done?'

'I haven't done anything,' said Alfie.

'So it *was* him,' said Old Bill. 'I knew it was. I might be old, Alfie Summerfield, but I've known your father since he was knee-high to a grasshopper and I could tell that was him walking past my window.'

'How did he seem?' asked Margie.

'Well, I don't know,' said Bill with a shrug. 'I only saw him through the net curtain. I've no way of telling, do I?'

'Where is he, Alfie?' asked Margie. 'Tell me!

Wait, is he upstairs? He is, isn't he? You have him upstairs in your bedroom! Georgie!' she cried, leaping from her chair and running out into the hallway, taking the stairs two at a time – something Alfie had never seen her do before. 'Georgie, are you up here?'

She ran into Alfie's bedroom, and he heard her opening the wardrobe and falling on the floor to look under the bed, and just at that moment there was another knock on the door and Alfie turned to stare at it for a moment before feeling a sense of relief. It was him – it had to be. He was safe. He'd come home. He reached for the latch and opened it, and for a moment he couldn't quite believe his eyes.

It wasn't Georgie Summerfield standing there.

It was Dr Ridgewell.

'You,' said Alfie in astonishment.

The doctor narrowed his eyes and frowned, as if he vaguely recognized the boy but couldn't remember where from. 'This is number twelve, isn't it?' he asked. 'Summerfield residence?'

'Yes,' said Alfie, the word catching in his throat.

'Is your mother home?'

'Alfie, who's at the door?'

Margie came back downstairs and opened the door wider, staring in disbelief at who was standing on her doorstep.

'Mrs Summerfield?' asked Dr Ridgewell.

'That's right.'

'May I come in? I'm Max Ridgewell. A doctor at the East Suffolk.'

'We've met,' said Margie. 'Half a dozen times at least.'

'We have?'

'Yes.'

Dr Ridgewell shook his head and had the good grace to look embarrassed. 'I'm sorry, Mrs Summerfield. There are so many people, you understand. Wives, mothers. I don't always remember everyone.'

'Come in,' said Margie, opening the door and ushering him into the parlour. 'This is my mother-in-law and my next-door neighbour, Mr Hemperton.'

'Good afternoon,' said Dr Ridgewell. 'Perhaps we should talk privately, Mrs Summerfield? There are some things that—'

'Anything you have to say to me you can say in front of these people,' said Margie quickly, waving her hand in the air and both embracing and dismissing them in the same gesture. 'Have you found him?'

Dr Ridgewell hesitated and looked surprised. 'You know he's gone missing, then?'

'I guessed. Bill thought he saw him earlier today. And Alfie here' – she nodded in the direction of her son – 'he's got something to do with it. Only he's not saying as yet. Are you, Alfie?'

Dr Ridgewell pointed a long bony finger in the air. 'I know you, don't I?' he said.

'No.'

'Yes I do. How do I know you? Your face is familiar to me.' He shook his head and he thought about it. 'Wait a minute,' he said after a moment. 'You're not . . . You're the boy with the shoeshine stand.'

'The what?' asked Margie.

'Down at King's Cross. That's you, isn't it?'

'No,' said Alfie, looking away.

'Yes it is!'

'Alfie, what's he talking about?' asked Margie. 'A shoeshine stand? You don't have a . . . The smell of polish,' she realized, shaking her head. 'In your bedroom. I'm always commenting on it.'

'All right, I shine shoes at the station,' admitted Alfie. 'But only to help us out. To help *you* out. I put the money in your purse. You take in washing! You take in darning! I'm doing my bit, like everyone else.'

'A shoeshine boy,' said Granny Summerfield, putting her hands on her face and looking thoroughly appalled. 'Have we sunk that low? What's become of us?'

'Look, can we leave this for now?' said Dr Ridgewell. 'I'm here about your husband, Mrs Summerfield. You realize he's gone missing? He's not at the hospital any more. And there are reports of a small boy hanging around the premises.'

'Alfie, where is he?' cried Margie, taking him by the shoulders. 'Tell me! He's not well. Don't you realize that? Your father's not well! Where have you—'

'I don't know!' shouted Alfie, bursting into tears now. 'I lost him.'

'You lost him?'

'He was with me at the station. I went over to buy him some cigarettes and then he disappeared. There was all this noise, you see. The slamming of doors. I think he was frightened and—'

'He can't abide loud noises,' said Dr Ridgewell. 'Most of them can't. It's all the shelling they had to put up with. It's played havoc with their nervous systems. That's why we try to keep the hospital as a place of peace and serenity. It's why we don't let children in to visit.'

'I didn't know he was going, did I?' snapped Margie. 'If I'd known, I never would have allowed it. But we have to look for him. He's out there somewhere. Who knows what harm he could come to? Bill, how about you and I—'

Just then there was yet another knock on the front door, and everyone turned round.

'I'll get it,' said Granny Summerfield, standing up and going into the hall. When she'd opened the front door, she slammed it shut again and marched directly back into the parlour.

'Well, who was it?' asked Margie.

'Nobody,' said Granny Summerfield. 'Now, Doctor, you were saying . . .?'

'It can't have been nobody!' cried Margie, and before Dr Ridgewell could speak again, there was another knock on the door.

'Ignore it!' cried Granny Summerfield.

'I will not ignore it!' said Margie, marching out of the room, her face growing red with fury. She opened the door, and there was Joe Patience, the conchie from number sixteen, standing outside.

'Joe,' said Margie with a sigh. 'It's not a good time.'

'He's sitting in my front room,' said Joe.

'Do not let that man into this house!' cried Granny Summerfield, storming out into the hallway now and staring at Joe Patience as if he was the devil incarnate. 'Shut it in his face, Margie!'

'Mrs Summerfield—' said Joe.

'Don't Mrs Summerfield me!' roared Granny Summerfield, rushing forward. 'Everything I did for you, Joe Patience! Everything I did! And how did you repay me? My son goes to war and you—'

'I couldn't!'

'Because you're a coward!'

'Because I won't hurt people! Like I was hurt!'

'Coward!'

'*Be quiet!*' roared Margie, looking at her

mother-in-law as if she might tear her limb from limb. 'Joe, what did you just say?'

'He's sitting in my front room,' repeated Joe.

'Who?' asked Granny Summerfield.

'Your son,' said Joe. 'Your husband,' he added, looking at Margie. 'Your dad,' he said, turning to Alfie, who was standing behind his mother and grandmother now. 'He's sitting in my front room.'

At first, no one moved. Then Margie ran. She broke past Joe and charged along to number sixteen, where the door was swinging open, and disappeared inside.

'What have you done?' asked Granny Summerfield, confused now, her voice filled with bewilderment.

'I haven't done anything,' said Joe. 'Alfie brought him home, didn't you, Alfie?'

Granny Summerfield turned to look at her grandson as Old Bill Hemperton and Dr Ridgewell stepped out into the hall.

'I wanted to save him,' said Alfie. 'That's all. You don't know what it was like there.'

'Alfie came to me,' said Joe, looking at Granny Summerfield. 'He told me what he was going to do. I suppose I should have told you. Or Margie. But I didn't think he'd go through with it. But then I saw them. And I wasn't sure what to do for the best. I couldn't come over. Georgie didn't look right – you understand that, don't you? I thought if I came over that I might cause more harm than good. So I waited. I followed them. Alfie took him to King's Cross. I watched them. And when he ran, I ran after him. I caught up with him. I took him for a drink, Elsie. And we had a chat. Just like old times. And then I brought him home.' He sighed. 'I think he's going to be all right, you know. If we all help him.'

There was a long silence, and Granny Summerfield's face softened. 'You ran after him,' she said quietly.

'Of course I did,' said Joe quietly. 'After everything you did for me? He's my oldest friend. Of course I ran after him.'

Granny Summerfield looked away. She hesitated for a few moments, and then she raised her left hand and reached out towards Joe's face, to the smooth burn marks that separated his hairline from his forehead. 'Joe,' she said. Nothing more.

'I'm sorry,' said Dr Ridgewell, stepping forward now. 'But your son . . . I need to see him.'

'Of course,' said Joe Patience, pulling back now, and as he did so Granny Summerfield stepped forward and linked her arm through his. 'He's over here. Come across, all of you.'

Joe, Dr Ridgewell, Granny Summerfield, Alfie and Old Bill Hemperton all made their way quick-smart to number sixteen and hurried inside, where they found Margie and Georgie sitting on the couch together, holding each other, their heads on each other's shoulders.

'Georgie!' cried Granny Summerfield, running forward and throwing her arms around both of them.

'Help me,' whispered Georgie, looking up at his mum and his wife. 'Help me. Please. Someone help me. My head . . .'

'Are you all right, Georgie lad?' asked Old Bill Hemperton, leaning forward.

'Mr Summerfield, it's me, Doctor Ridgewell.'

'Dad!'

Alfie fought his way through and buried his body against his father's, locking his arms around his waist, pushing everyone else aside. A moment later, a great noise built from outside in the street, and everyone, except Alfie and Georgie, turned their heads to look out of the window.

'What on earth . . . ?' asked Old Bill Hemperton, watching as all the doors began opening and the people from the houses opposite came out and started crying and hugging each other. 'What's going on out there?'

'Stay here,' said Margie, opening the front door, and as she did so, Helena Morris from number eighteen and Mrs Tamorin from number twenty ran past.

'What's happening?' shouted Margie. 'What's going on out here? Why all the fuss?'

'It's over!' said Mrs Tamorin. 'Haven't you heard? The war's over. We won.'

On the sofa, Georgie's eyes closed tight and tears started to stream down his face as he wrapped his arms tighter around his son, holding him in a close embrace.

The war was over at last.

And there was still six weeks to go to Christmas.

14

TAKE ME BACK TO DEAR OLD BLIGHTY

Kalena Janáček looked into the front parlour of her home at number six Damley Road and found her father sitting in an armchair with a newspaper open on the floor beneath him. On his left sat an open shoeshine box made of dark brown mahogany wood, twice as long as it was wide, with a gold-coloured clasp to unlock the lid from the base. Carved into the side was the word *Holzknecht*, and an emblem that displayed an eagle soaring above a mountain, wild-eyed and dangerous.

Mr Janáček was shining his shoes.

'Do you have the present?' she asked, and her father nodded, pointing towards the table, where a copy of *Great Expectations* by Charles Dickens sat. It was July 1922, almost four years since the end of the war, and Alfie Summerfield was having a thirteenth birthday party.

'We should go,' said Mr Janáček, putting his shoes on and standing up. He reached for his cane

– the one that he'd bought when he first came back from the Isle of Man; the same one that helped him make his way from number six to the sweet shop and back again. His leg had been fine before he left, of course; this was something that had happened to him inside the camp. 'Should we tell them our news today or wait?' he asked. *Should we tell zem our news today or vait?*

'Not today,' said Kalena, shaking her head. 'Let's wait until after Alfie's birthday. We'll tell them tomorrow.'

'All right. I should take the sign down, though, I suppose,' he said as they left the house. He looked down the street towards the sweet shop, which had had a FOR SALE sign on it ever since he and his daughter had been despatched back to London, like redirected post, in 1919. The neighbours all thought it was for show, that the Janáčeks would never leave, but they had agreed between them that once the internment was over they would leave England for ever and never return. It had just taken this long to sell the shop.

'When will we go, anyway?' asked Kalena.

'It will take a couple of weeks for the legal work to be completed. All being well, we should be back in Prague by the end of the month. And that day can't come soon enough as far as I'm concerned.'

'Won't you miss London at all?' she asked, linking arms with him, and he shook his head.

'Why should I miss it?' he asked. 'It is not home. It was never home. I thought it was but I was wrong. If I never see England again, it will be too soon. You feel the same way, don't you?'

Kalena hesitated. She wanted to leave, of course. She had been born in this country and then been treated like an outsider and she could not forgive them for that. But she remembered that she had been happy before the war, that she had had many friends, the best one of all being Alfie.

'Can you believe that it was eight years ago today that we stood inside this house and lamented the outbreak of the war?' asked Mr Janáček, knocking on the Summerfields' front door. 'And yet it feels like a hundred years ago, don't you agree? Nothing now is as it was.' *Nussing now is as it vas.* 'Everything seems like an illusion to me. I did nothing wrong. And these people have destroyed me. No, we will go back to Prague, you and I. We will be safe there.'

Granny Summerfield stood in the kitchen of number eleven and pressed her finger against the top of the sponge cake that she had baked that morning. It was cool to the touch. She opened the fridge and took out the icing that she had made earlier. Flour, sugar, milk, cream; it still felt strange to her to have such ready access to these things again after so many years of being unable to find them. Not that they were readily available, of course. You had to know where to go and you had to keep 'in' with some of the shopkeepers. But still, things were much better than they had been during the war. Things were getting back to normal, and everyone said that this was the war to end all wars; they would never see its like again.

She had always enjoyed baking, and one of the greatest hardships for her during those years had been her inability to prepare her favourite food and share it with the people she loved. She remembered when she was a girl and had first learned how to cook – what an adventure it had seemed! Now, of course, she did more cooking than she ever had before, even though she was getting on a bit. Margie didn't have much time on her hands, what with all the changes that had taken place across the road at number twelve, but she didn't mind; she liked to help out.

She sat down, sure that she had everything ready for the party later, and settled into her armchair for forty winks just as Old Bill Hemperton across the road struck up his gramophone and the first melancholy strings of a new record he'd bought began to play across the street. In the old days, of course, Granny Summerfield would have been across the road like a shot, banging on his door and telling him to turn that racket down, but she didn't do that any more. Life was too short.

And besides, she quite liked this song.

Margie checked her watch and gasped a little under her breath. She'd been hoping to finish at the hospital at lunch time in order to get everything ready for Alfie's party, and here it was, almost one o'clock already, and no sign of her leaving.

'Nurse Summerfield!'

She turned round and saw Matron walking towards her, her arms swishing back and forth as she strode along.

'Yes, Matron?'

'I know you wanted to go home early today but I wondered if you might be able to stay a little longer?'

Margie shook her head. 'I can't. I would if I could, but it's my son's birthday. I promised I'd be home.'

'Of course, of course,' said Matron, a frown crossing her face. 'I wouldn't ask, only . . .'

Margie sighed. She'd been working at the hospital for five years now and sometimes couldn't quite believe that she had never left after the war. But then, she had never thought about leaving. She found the work interesting and she liked helping people. And things were different now, anyway. It wasn't like the old days, when a married woman going out to work would have been frowned upon.

Things were starting to change for the better.

'What's happened?' she asked.

'It's just a young man who's been brought in,' explained Matron. 'He's in a bad way, poor fellow. He must have taken a notion last night and did something stupid. He'll survive, certainly, but we're just waiting for his parents to get here. I thought maybe you might sit with him for a while.'

'How old is he?' asked Margie quietly.

'About twenty-seven, I should think.'

Margie nodded. She knew what that meant. 'Where is he?'

'He's in St Agatha's Ward. Bed three. I spoke to his father; he'll be here in half an hour. You can go once he arrives. You don't mind, do you?'

Margie smiled and shook her head. 'No,' she said. 'No, I don't mind.'

She made her way towards St Agatha's Ward and went in. It wasn't difficult to see which bed Matron had been referring to. The man was lying on his side, tears streaming down his face. When he saw Margie walking towards him, he pulled his arms out of sight, underneath the blankets, but not before she had glimpsed the tight bandages wrapped around his wrists. She pulled a chair over and glanced up at the name above the bed – Cecil Cratchley – before smiling at him and laying her hand on his shoulder.

'Hello, Cecil,' she said.

The young man blinked a few times but said not a word.

'I'm Nurse Summerfield,' she continued. 'I'm going to sit with you for a little while, if that's all right. I think your parents are coming in to see you. And then we're going to take good care of you, all of us here at the hospital, and your mum and dad, and we're going to sort everything out. And before you know it you'll be right as rain again. Do you hear me, Cecil? You're going to be right as rain, and you'll look back on these days in the future and wonder what you were so upset about. Everything, Cecil, is going to be all right.'

And somehow the young man seemed to believe her, because he looked up and gave a little smile as he locked eyes with her. And Margie smiled right back. She was good at this. The truth was, she had finally found something that she was good at.

Mr Asquith trotted happily along Damley Close, his tail swishing sporadically to keep the flies away. He'd never been thrilled about being attached to a milk float, but a life was a life, and one did what one had to do to get along. And anyway, at least that clown Henry Lyons had been despatched elsewhere and his pal, his true old pal – where had he been? – was back at the helm. There were worse ways to make a living, he supposed.

The final milk churns were delivered to Damley Close just after one o'clock in the afternoon, and now that the float was empty, Georgie Summerfield began to make the journey back to the dairy, lighting up a cigarette with a half-frown on his face. 'Do you know,' he said, 'I'm thinking of giving these things up. They can't be much good for you, can they?'

Alfie shrugged. He did a lot of shrugging these days. Margie said it was his age. Georgie didn't mind. He knew that his son was growing older. If that was the worst of it, then they wouldn't have got off too badly.

'Do you remember when you used to beg me to let you ride the float with me, son?' he asked, and Alfie smiled, for this was a good memory.

'And you never used to let me,' he said.

'Well, you were too young,' said Georgie. 'The trouble I would have got into! The dairy would have gone mad if they'd found out, and that's nothing to what your mother would have done. I didn't dare, Alfie! Didn't have the nerve!'

Alfie shook his head and looked across at his father. 'You had nerve,' he said quietly. 'I know that much, anyway.'

Georgie nodded and slowed down as Joe Patience emerged from the library on the right-hand side of the street. He tooted the horn, and Joe looked up in surprise but gave a wave when he saw Georgie and Alfie seated side by side on the milk float.

'He's doing well for himself these days all the same, isn't he?' said Georgie, waving back. 'Every bookshop I pass, there's that book of his in the window. I keep meaning to buy a copy and read it but I don't think I could concentrate that long.'

'You can borrow my copy if you want,' said Alfie.

'You've read it, then?'

'Yes.'

'And what's it like?'

Alfie smiled. 'Dirty,' he said, which made Georgie burst out laughing.

'Maybe I will have a read of it after all,' he said, shaking his head. 'Only not a word to your mother, do you hear? What time is it now, anyway?'

Alfie glanced at his watch. 'Almost half past one,' he said.

'Perfect,' said Georgie. 'We'll get the float back, give Mr Asquith a wash down, then be home in time to change before the guests arrive.' He whistled through his teeth for a moment. 'Thirteen years old,' he mused. 'Makes me feel old, that does. I can't believe how grown up you've become. Are you looking forward to your party?'

Alfie said nothing, and Georgie turned to look at him in surprise.

'You're not, are you? I can see it in your face.'

'It's not that,' said Alfie. 'I don't think I really like birthdays, to be honest.'

'What? But everyone likes birthdays!'

'I don't,' said Alfie. 'It makes me think of what it was like to be five again. And then what it was like to be six, seven, eight and nine.'

Georgie nodded and steered Mr Asquith to the left. 'Those days are all in the past now, son,' he said. 'We have happy times ahead of us. These last few years have been good, haven't they? I know it took me a while to . . . well, to get better. But I'm fine these days, amn't I? I'm sleeping, I'm eating, I'm working.'

'You still have nightmares,' said Alfie quietly.

'But not as many as before. Honestly, Alfie, I'm fine. There's nothing for you to worry about. And look, here we are on a fine summer's day, father and son riding the milk float together like you always wanted. It's not a bad life really, is it?'

Alfie smiled and shook his head. 'No,' he said. 'No, it's a pretty good life, all told.'

They drove along in silence for a few minutes, and only when the dairy came into sight did Georgie speak again.

'I don't think . . . I don't think I've ever really thanked you, have I, Alfie?'

'For what?'

'For succeeding in your secret mission,' said

Georgie with a smile. 'For coming to find me in the hospital. For breaking me out.'

'It wasn't very sensible when I look back on it,' said Alfie.

'No, but it all came good in the end. And it meant everything to me to see you. To know the lengths you'd go to in order to get me back home again. That's what kept all of us alive in the trenches, you know. The idea that one day we'd get to go home again. And see our wives and our children. You're what kept me alive, even at the lowest points.'

Alfie turned away and watched as the houses passed by on the left-hand side. He didn't really like to talk about the old days; he was just happy they were behind them all and life had got back to normal. Or a new type of normal, anyway.

'I never knew what you had in mind,' said Georgie. 'All the trouble you could have got in to, all the chances you took, all that hard work with Mr Janáček's shoeshine box. All the sacrifices you made. Taking trains on your own when you'd never been on a train in your life. Coming to find me, bringing me home, saving me. I never knew why you thought you should do it all.'

He turned into the dairy and pulled Mr Asquith to a halt. It was dark in here and he turned to look at his son, his Alfie, who was wondering whether he'd get to ride on the float with his dad again the following day.

'Tell me, son,' said Georgie. 'Why did you go to so much trouble?'

Alfie turned and stared at his father. He opened his mouth to speak but the words wouldn't come. There were so many memories in his head – things that sometimes kept him awake at night, things that sometimes gave him nightmares just like Georgie's. The worry when his dad went missing. The stench of the hospital. The shaking and trembling of the patients. The way they spoke, the nonsense of it. These were things he would never forget, things that would influence the man he would one day become.

'Why, son?' repeated Georgie.

Alfie shook his head and turned away, shrugging his shoulders for the hundredth time that day. He couldn't tell his father the reason. Not just yet. Maybe when he was older he'd be able to say the words. He already knew them, after all. Mr Janáček had said them to him a long time ago.

He'd done it for the best reason in the world. For love.

Discussion points for book clubs:

1. Send Me Away With a Smile

- Each chapter of the story opens with a line from a song that was popular or famous during the time the book is set, such as *Send Me Away With a Smile, Keep the Home Fires Burning* and *Oh! It's a Lovely War.* What do you think these lines add to the story?

- Are there any lines that fit their chapters especially well? Why?

- Why do you think war-related songs were so popular at this time? Do you think a similar song about any modern-day conflicts might ever be as popular today?

2. Georgie and Joe

- Despite having been begged not to sign up as a soldier the day war breaks out, Georgie Summerfield arrives home in his new uniform the very next day. Why do you think he's so quick to do this?

- If you had been eligible to become a soldier for your country on that day, do you think you'd have behaved the same way? Does what you now know about the conditions soldiers faced in this war make any difference to your choice?

- What do you think of Joe's point of view? Do you think the way he was treated by other people for his decision not to fight was ever right? Should others have respected his view and allowed him to make his own choice, or do those things count for less in a wartime situation?

3. Alfie's Understanding

- Throughout the book, Alfie knows and understands a certain amount of what is happening around him, while other things don't make sense to him. As we are seeing the story through Alfie's eyes, what effect does this have on the reader?
- We learn that Margie has kept a lot of the truth hidden from Alfie, including Georgie's later letters. Do you think she was right to do this?

4. Kalena

- When Alfie tells his parents that Kalena wants to be Prime Minister when she is older, they laugh at the idea. Things have changed a great deal since the 1930s, but do you think there may still be people who would have a similar reaction today? Do we have complete equality between men and women?

Read on for an extract of

The Boy in the Striped Pyjamas

Chapter One

Bruno Makes a Discovery

One afternoon, when Bruno came home from school, he was surprised to find Maria, the family's maid – who always kept her head bowed and never looked up from the carpet – standing in his bedroom, pulling all his belongings out of the wardrobe and packing them in four large wooden crates, even the things he'd hidden at the back that belonged to him and were nobody else's business.

'What are you doing?' he asked in as polite a tone as he could muster, for although he wasn't happy to come home and find someone going through his possessions, his mother had always told him that he was to treat Maria respectfully and not just imitate the way Father spoke to her. 'You take your hands off my things.'

Maria shook her head and pointed towards the staircase behind him, where Bruno's mother had just appeared. She was a tall woman with long red hair that she bundled into a sort of net behind her head, and she was twisting her hands together nervously as if there was something she didn't want to have to say or something she didn't want to have to believe.

'Mother,' said Bruno, marching towards her, 'what's going on? Why is Maria going through my things?'

'She's packing them,' explained Mother.

'Packing them?' he asked, running quickly through the events of the previous few days to consider whether he'd been particularly naughty or had used those words out loud that he wasn't allowed to use and was being sent away because of it. He couldn't think of anything though. In fact over the last few days he had behaved in a perfectly decent manner to everyone and couldn't remember causing any chaos at all. 'Why?' he asked then. 'What have I done?'

Mother had walked into her own bedroom by then but Lars, the butler, was in there, packing her things too. She sighed and threw her hands in the air in frustration before marching back to the staircase, followed by Bruno, who wasn't going to let the matter drop without an explanation.

'Mother,' he insisted. 'What's going on? Are we moving?'

'Come downstairs with me,' said Mother, leading the way towards the large dining room where the Fury had been to dinner the week before. 'We'll talk down there.'

Bruno ran downstairs and even passed her out on the staircase so that he was waiting in the dining room when she arrived. He looked at her without saying anything for a moment and thought to himself that she couldn't have applied her make-up correctly that morning because the rims of her eyes were more red than usual, like his own after he'd been causing chaos and got into trouble and ended up crying.

'Now, you don't have to worry, Bruno,' said Mother, sitting down in the chair where the beautiful blonde woman who had come to dinner with the Fury had sat and waved at him when Father closed the doors. 'In fact if anything it's going to be a great adventure.'

'What is?' he asked. 'Am I being sent away?'

'No, not just you,' she said, looking as if she might smile for a moment but thinking better of it. 'We all are. Your father and I, Gretel and you. All four of us.'

Bruno thought about this and frowned. He wasn't particularly bothered if Gretel was being sent away because she was a Hopeless Case and caused nothing but trouble for him. But it seemed a little unfair that they all had to go with her.

'But where?' he asked. 'Where are we going exactly? Why can't we stay here?'

'Your father's job,' explained Mother. 'You know how important it is, don't you?'

'Yes, of course,' said Bruno, nodding his head, because there were always so many visitors to the house – men in fantastic uniforms, women with typewriters that he had to keep his mucky hands off – and they were always very polite to Father and told each other that he was a man to watch and that the Fury had big things in mind for him.

'Well, sometimes when someone is very important,' continued Mother, 'the man who employs him asks him to go somewhere else because there's a very special job that needs doing there.'

'What kind of job?' asked Bruno, because if he was honest with himself – which he always tried to be – he wasn't entirely sure what job Father did.

In school they had talked about their fathers one day and Karl had said that his father was a greengrocer, which Bruno knew to be true because he ran the greengrocer's shop in the centre of town. And Daniel had said that his father was a teacher, which Bruno knew to be true because he taught the big boys who it was always wise to steer clear of. And Martin had said that his father was a chef, which Bruno knew to be true because he sometimes collected Martin from school and when he did he always wore a white smock and a tartan apron, as if he'd just stepped out of his kitchen.

But when they asked Bruno what his father did he opened his mouth to tell them, then realized that he didn't know himself. All he could say was that his father was a man to watch and that the Fury had big things in mind for him. Oh, and that he had a fantastic uniform too.

'It's a very important job,' said Mother, hesitating for a moment. 'A job that needs a very special man to do it. You can understand that, can't you?'

'And we all have to go too?' asked Bruno.

'Of course we do,' said Mother. 'You wouldn't want Father to go to his new job on his own and be lonely there, would you?'

'I suppose not,' said Bruno.

'Father would miss us all terribly if we weren't with him,' she added.

'Who would he miss the most?' asked Bruno. 'Me or Gretel?'

'He would miss you both equally,' said Mother, for she was a great believer in not playing favourites, which Bruno respected, especially since he knew that he was her favourite really.

'But what about our house?' asked Bruno. 'Who's going to take care of it while we're gone?'

Mother sighed and looked around the room as if she might never see it again. It was a very beautiful house and had five floors in total, if you included the basement, where Cook made all the food and Maria and Lars sat at the table arguing with each other and calling each other names that you weren't supposed to use. And if you added in the little room at the top of the house with the slanted windows where Bruno could see right across Berlin if he stood up on his tiptoes and held onto the frame tightly.

'We have to close up the house for now,' said Mother. 'But we'll come back to it someday.'

'And what about Cook?' asked Bruno. 'And Lars? And Maria? Are they not going to live in it?'

'They're coming with us,' explained Mother. 'But that's enough questions for now. Maybe you should go upstairs and help Maria with your packing.'

Bruno stood up from the seat but didn't go anywhere. There were just a few more questions he needed to put to her before he could allow the matter to be settled.

'And how far away is it?' he asked. 'The new job, I mean. Is it further than a mile away?'

'Oh my,' said Mother with a laugh, although it was a strange kind of laugh because she didn't look happy and turned away from Bruno as if she didn't want him to see her face. 'Yes, Bruno,' she said. 'It's more than a mile away. Quite a lot more than that, in fact.'

Bruno's eyes opened wide and his mouth made the shape of an O. He felt his arms stretching out at his sides like they did whenever something surprised him. 'You don't mean we're leaving Berlin?' he asked, gasping for air as he got the words out.

'I'm afraid so,' said Mother, nodding her head sadly. 'Your father's job is—'

'But what about school?' said Bruno, interrupting her, a thing he knew he was not supposed to do but which he felt he would be forgiven for on this occasion. 'And what about Karl and Daniel and Martin? How will they know where I am when we want to do things together?'

'You'll have to say goodbye to your friends for the time being,' said Mother. 'Although I'm sure you'll see them again in time. And don't interrupt your mother when she's talking, please,' she added, for although this was strange and unpleasant news, there was certainly no need for Bruno to break the rules of politeness which he had been taught.

'Say goodbye to them?' he asked, staring at her in surprise. 'Say goodbye to them?' he repeated, spluttering out the words as if his mouth was full of biscuits that he'd munched into tiny pieces but not actually swallowed yet. 'Say goodbye to Karl and Daniel and Martin?' he continued, his voice coming dangerously close to shouting, which was not allowed indoors. 'But they're my three best friends for life!'

'Oh, you'll make other friends,' said Mother,

waving her hand in the air dismissively, as if the making of a boy's three best friends for life was an easy thing.

'But we had plans,' he protested.

'Plans?' asked Mother, raising an eyebrow. 'What sort of plans?'

'Well, that would be telling,' said Bruno, who could not reveal the exact nature of the plans – which included causing a lot of chaos, especially in a few weeks' time when school finished for the summer holidays and they didn't have to spend all their time just making plans but could actually put them into effect instead.

'I'm sorry, Bruno,' said Mother, 'but your plans are just going to have to wait. We don't have a choice in this.'

'But, Mother!'

'Bruno, that's enough,' she said, snapping at him now and standing up to show him that she was serious when she said that was enough. 'Honestly, only last week you were complaining about how much things have changed here recently.'

'Well, I don't like the way we have to turn all the lights off at night now,' he admitted.

'Everyone has to do that,' said Mother. 'It keeps us safe. And who knows, maybe we'll be in less danger if we move away. Now, I need you to go upstairs and help Maria with your packing. We don't have as much time to prepare as I would have liked, thanks to some people.'

Bruno nodded and walked away sadly, knowing that 'some people' was a grown-up's word for 'Father' and one that he wasn't supposed to use himself.

He made his way up the stairs slowly, holding onto the banister with one hand, and wondered whether the new house in the new place where the new job was would have as fine a banister to slide down as this one did. For the banister in this house stretched from the very top floor – just outside the little room where, if he stood on his tiptoes and held onto the frame of the window tightly, he could see right across Berlin – to the ground floor, just in front of the two enormous oak doors. And Bruno liked nothing better than to get on board the banister at the top floor and slide his way through the house, making whooshing sounds as he went.

Down from the top floor to the next one, where Mother and Father's room was, and the large bathroom, and where he wasn't supposed to be in any case.

Down to the next floor, where his own room was, and Gretel's room too, and the smaller bathroom which he was supposed to use more often than he really did.

Down to the ground floor, where you fell off the end of the banister and had to land flat on your two feet or it was five points against you and you had to start all over again.

The banister was the best thing about this house – that and the fact that Grandfather and Grandmother lived so near by – and when he thought about that it made him wonder whether they were coming to the new job too and he presumed that they were because they could hardly be left behind. No one needed Gretel much because she was a Hopeless Case – it would be a lot easier if she stayed to look after the house – but Grandfather and Grandmother? Well, that was an entirely different matter.

Bruno went up the stairs slowly towards his room, but before going inside he looked back down towards the ground floor and saw Mother entering Father's office, which faced the dining room – and was Out Of Bounds At All Times And No Exceptions – and he heard her speaking loudly to him until Father spoke louder than Mother could and that put a stop to their conversation. Then the door of the office closed and Bruno couldn't hear any more so he thought it would be a good idea if he went back to his room and took over the packing from Maria, because otherwise she might pull all his belongings out of the wardrobe without any care or consideration, even the things he'd hidden at the back that belonged to him and were nobody else's business.

Chapter Two

The New House

When he first saw their new house Bruno's eyes opened wide, his mouth made the shape of an O and his arms stretched out at his sides once again. Everything about it seemed to be the exact opposite of their old home and he couldn't believe that they were really going to live there.

The house in Berlin had stood on a quiet street and alongside it were a handful of other big houses like his own, and it was always nice to look at them because they were almost the same as his house but not quite, and other boys lived in them who he played with (if they were friends) or steered clear of (if they were trouble). The new house, however, stood all on its own in an empty, desolate place and there were no other houses anywhere to be seen, which meant there would be no other families around and no other boys to play with, neither friends nor trouble.

The house in Berlin was enormous, and even

though he'd lived there for nine years he was still able to find nooks and crannies that he hadn't fully finished exploring yet. There were even whole rooms – such as Father's office, which was Out Of Bounds At All Times And No Exceptions – that he had barely been inside. However, the new house had only three floors: a top floor where all three bedrooms were and only one bathroom, a ground floor with a kitchen, a dining room and a new office for Father (which, he presumed, had the same restrictions as the old one), and a basement where the servants slept.

All around the house in Berlin were other streets of large houses, and when you walked towards the centre of town there were always people strolling along and stopping to chat to each other or rushing around and saying they had no time to stop, not today, not when they had a hundred and one things to do. There were shops with bright store fronts, and fruit and vegetable stalls with big trays piled high with cabbages, carrots, cauliflowers and corn. Some were overspilling with leeks and mushrooms, turnips and sprouts; others with lettuce and green beans, courgettes and parsnips. Sometimes he liked to stand in front of these stalls and close his eyes and breathe in their aromas, feeling his head grow dizzy with the mixed scents of sweetness and life. But there were no other streets around the new house, no one strolling along or rushing around, and definitely no shops or fruit and vegetable stalls. When he closed his eyes, everything around him just felt empty and cold, as if he was in the loneliest place in the world. The middle of nowhere.

In Berlin there had been tables set out on the street, and sometimes when he walked home from school with Karl, Daniel and Martin there would be men and women sitting at them, drinking frothy drinks and laughing loudly; the people who sat at these tables must be very funny people, he always thought, because it didn't matter what they said, somebody always laughed. But there was something about the new house that made Bruno think that no one ever laughed there; that there was nothing to laugh at and nothing to be happy about.

'I think this was a bad idea,' said Bruno a few hours after they arrived, while Maria was unpacking his suitcases upstairs. (Maria wasn't the only maid at the new house either: there were three others who were quite skinny and only ever spoke to each other in whispering voices. There was an old man too who, he was told, was there to prepare the vegetables every day and wait on them at the dinner table, and who looked very unhappy but also a little angry.)

'We don't have the luxury of thinking,' said Mother, opening a box that contained the set of sixty-four glasses that Grandfather and Grandmother had given her when she married Father. 'Some people make all the decisions for us.'

Bruno didn't know what she meant by that so he pretended that she'd never said it at all. 'I think this was a bad idea,' he repeated. 'I think the best thing to do would be to forget all about this and just go back home. We can chalk it up to experience,' he added, a phrase he had learned recently and was determined to use as often as possible.

Mother smiled and put the glasses down carefully on the table. 'I have another phrase for you,' she said. 'It's that we have to make the best of a bad situation.'

'Well, I don't know that we do,' said Bruno. 'I think you should just tell Father that you've changed your mind and, well, if we have to stay here for the rest of the day and have dinner here this evening and sleep here tonight because we're all tired, then that's all right, but we should probably get up early in the morning if we're to make it back to Berlin by tea-time tomorrow.'

Mother sighed. 'Bruno, why don't you just go upstairs and help Maria unpack?' she asked.

'But there's no point unpacking if we're only going to—'

'Bruno, just do it, please!' snapped Mother, because apparently it was all right if she interrupted him but it didn't work the other way round. 'We're here, we've arrived, this is our home for the foreseeable future and we just have to make the best of things. Do you understand me?'

He didn't understand what the 'foreseeable future' meant and told her so.

'It means that this is where we live now, Bruno,' said Mother. 'And that's an end to it.'

Bruno had a pain in his stomach and he could feel something growing inside him, something that when it worked its way up from the lowest depths inside him to the outside world would either make him shout and scream that the whole thing was wrong and unfair and a big mistake for which somebody would pay one of these days, or just make him burst into tears instead. He couldn't understand how this had all come about. One day he was perfectly content, playing at home, having three best friends for life, sliding down banisters, trying to stand on his tiptoes to see right across Berlin, and now he was stuck here in this cold, nasty house with three whispering maids and a waiter who was both unhappy and angry, where no one looked as if they could ever be cheerful again.

'Bruno, I want you to go upstairs and unpack and I want you to do it now,' said Mother in an unfriendly voice, and he knew that she meant business so he turned round and marched away without another word. He could feels tears springing up behind his eyes but he was determined that he wouldn't allow them to appear.

He went upstairs and turned slowly around in a full circle, hoping he might find a small door or cubby hole where a decent amount of exploration could eventually be done, but there wasn't one. On his floor there were just four doors, two on either side, facing each other. A door into his room, a door into Gretel's room, a door into Mother and Father's room, and a door into the bathroom.

'This isn't home and it never will be,' he muttered under his breath as he went through his own door to find all his clothes scattered on the bed and the boxes of toys and books not even unpacked yet. It was obvious that Maria did not have her priorities right.

'Mother sent me to help,' he said quietly, and Maria nodded and pointed towards a big bag that contained all his socks and vests and underpants.

'If you sort that lot out, you could put them in the chest of drawers over there,' she said, pointing towards an ugly chest that stood across the room beside a mirror that was covered in dust.

Bruno sighed and opened the bag; it was full to the brim with his underwear and he wanted nothing more than to crawl inside it and hope that when he climbed out again he'd have woken up and be back home again.

'What do you think of all this, Maria?' he asked after a long silence because he had always liked Maria and felt as if she was one of the family, even though Father said she was just a maid and overpaid at that.

'All what?' she asked.

'This,' he said as if it was the most obvious thing in the world. 'Coming to a place like this. Don't you think we've made a big mistake?'

'That's not for me to say, Master Bruno,' said Maria. 'Your mother has explained to you about your father's job and—'

'Oh, I'm tired of hearing about Father's job,' said Bruno, interrupting her. 'That's all we ever hear about, if you ask me. Father's job this and Father's job that. Well, if Father's job means that we have to move away from our house and the sliding banister and my three best friends for life, then I think Father should think twice about his job, don't you?'

Just at that moment there was a creak outside in the hallway and Bruno looked up to see the door of Mother and Father's room opening slightly. He froze, unable to move for a moment. Mother was still downstairs, which meant that Father was in there and he might have heard everything that Bruno had just said. He watched the door, hardly daring to breathe, wondering whether Father might come through it and take him downstairs for a serious talking-to.

The door opened wider and Bruno stepped back as a figure appeared, but it wasn't Father. It was a much younger man, and not as tall as Father either, but he wore the same type of uniform, only without as many decorations on it. He looked very serious and his cap was secured tightly on his head. Around his temples Bruno could see that he had very blond hair, an almost unnatural shade of yellow. He was carrying a box in his hands and walking towards the staircase, but he stopped for a moment when he saw Bruno standing there watching him. He looked the boy up and down as if he had never seen a child before and wasn't quite sure what he was supposed to do with one: eat it, ignore it or kick it down the stairs. Instead he gave Bruno a quick nod and continued on his way.

'Who was that?' asked Bruno. The young man had seemed so serious and busy that he assumed he must be someone very important.

'One of your father's soldiers, I suppose,' said Maria, who had stood up very straight when the young man appeared and held her hands before her like a person in prayer. She had stared down at the ground rather than at his face, as if she was afraid she might be turned to stone if she looked directly at him; she only relaxed when he had gone. 'We'll get to know them in time.'

'I don't think I like him,' said Bruno. 'He was too serious.'

'Your father is very serious too,' said Maria.

'Yes, but he's Father,' explained Bruno. 'Fathers are supposed to be serious. It doesn't matter whether they're greengrocers or teachers or chefs or commandants,' he said, listing all the jobs that he knew decent, respectable fathers did and whose titles he had thought about a thousand times. 'And I don't think that man looked like a father. Although he was very serious, that's for sure.'

'Well, they have very serious jobs,' said Maria with a sigh. 'Or so they think anyway. But if I was you I'd steer clear of the soldiers.'

'I don't see what else there is to do other than that,' said Bruno sadly. 'I don't even think there's going to be anyone to play with other than Gretel, and what fun is that after all? She's a Hopeless Case.'

He felt as if he was about to cry again but stopped himself, not wanting to look like a baby in front of Maria. He looked around the room without fully lifting his eyes up from the ground, trying to see whether there was anything of interest to be found. There wasn't. Or there didn't seem to be. But then one thing caught his eye. Over in the corner of the room opposite the door there was a window in the ceiling that stretched down into the wall, a little like the one on the top floor of the house in Berlin, only not so high. Bruno looked at it and thought that he might be able to see out without even having to stand on tiptoes.

He walked slowly towards it, hoping that from here he might be able to see all the way back to Berlin and his house and the streets around it and the tables where the people sat and drank their frothy drinks and told each other hilarious stories. He walked slowly because he didn't want to be disappointed. But it was just a small boy's room and there was only so far he could walk before he arrived at the window. He put his face to the glass and saw what was out there, and this time when his eyes opened wide and his mouth made the shape of an O, his hands stayed by his sides because something made him feel very cold and unsafe.

Chapter Three

The Hopeless Case

Bruno was sure that it would have made a lot more sense if they had left Gretel behind in Berlin to look after the house because she was nothing but trouble. In fact he had heard her described on any number of occasions as being Trouble From Day One.

Gretel was three years older than Bruno and she had made it clear to him from as far back as he could remember that when it came to the ways of the world, particularly any events within that world that concerned the two of them, she was in charge. Bruno didn't like to admit that he was a little scared of her, but if he was honest with himself – which he always tried to be – he would have admitted that he was.

She had some nasty habits, as was to be expected from sisters. She spent far too long in the bathroom in the mornings for one thing, and didn't seem to mind if Bruno was left outside, hopping from foot to foot, desperate to go.

She had a large collection of dolls positioned

on shelves around her room that stared at Bruno when he went inside and followed him around, watching whatever he did. He was sure that if he went exploring in her room when she was out of the house, they would report back to her on everything he did. She had some very unpleasant friends too, who seemed to think that it was clever to make fun of him, a thing he never would have done if he had been three years older than her. All Gretel's unpleasant friends seemed to enjoy nothing more than torturing him and said nasty things to him whenever Mother or Maria were nowhere in sight.

'Bruno's not nine, he's only six,' said one particular monster over and over again in a singsong voice, dancing around him and poking him in the ribs.

'I'm not six, I'm nine,' he protested, trying to get away.

'Then why are you so small?' asked the monster. 'All the other nine-year-olds are bigger than you.'

This was true, and a particular sore point for Bruno. It was a source of constant disappointment to him that he wasn't as tall as any of the other boys in his class. In fact he only came up to their shoulders. Whenever he walked along the streets with Karl, Daniel and Martin, people sometimes mistook him for the younger brother of one of them when in fact he was the second oldest.

'So you must be only six,' insisted the monster, and Bruno would run away and do his stretching exercises and hope that he would wake up one morning and have grown an extra foot or two.

So one good thing about not being in Berlin any more was the fact that none of them would be around to torture him. Perhaps if he was forced to stay at the new house for a while, even as long as a month, he would have grown by the time they returned home and then they wouldn't be able to be mean to him any more. It was something to keep in mind anyway if he wanted to do what Mother had suggested and make the best of a bad situation.

He ran into Gretel's room without knocking and discovered her placing her civilization of dolls on various shelves around the room.

'What are you doing in here?' she shouted, spinning round. 'Don't you know you don't enter a lady's room without knocking?'

'You didn't bring all your dolls with you, surely?' asked Bruno, who had developed a habit of ignoring most of his sister's questions and asking a few of his own in their place.

'Of course I did,' she replied. 'You don't think I'd have left them at home? Why, it could be weeks before we're back there again.'

'Weeks?' said Bruno, sounding disappointed but secretly pleased because he'd resigned himself to the idea of spending a month there. 'Do you really think so?'

'Well, I asked Father and he said we would be here for the foreseeable future.'

'What is the foreseeable future exactly?' asked Bruno, sitting down on the side of her bed.

'It means weeks from now,' said Gretel with an intelligent nod of her head. 'Perhaps as long as three.'

'That's all right then,' said Bruno. 'As long as it's just for the foreseeable future and not for a month. I hate it here.'

Gretel looked at her little brother and found herself agreeing with him for once. 'I know what you mean,' she said. 'It's not very nice, is it?'

'It's horrible,' said Bruno.

'Well, yes,' said Gretel, acknowledging that. 'It's horrible right now. But once the house is smartened up a bit it probably won't seem so bad. I heard Father say that whoever lived here at Out-With before us lost their job very quickly and didn't have time to make the place nice for us.'

'Out-With?' asked Bruno. 'What's an Out-With?'

'It's not *an* Out-With, Bruno,' said Gretel with a sigh. 'It's just Out-With.'

'Well, what's Out-With then?' he repeated. 'Out with what?'

'That's the name of the house,' explained Gretel. 'Out-With.'

Bruno considered this. He hadn't seen any sign on the outside to say that was what it was called, nor had he seen any writing on the front door. His own house back in Berlin didn't even have a name; it was just called number four.

'But what does it mean?' he asked in exasperation. 'Out with what?'

'Out with the people who lived here before us, I expect,' said Gretel. 'It must have to do with the fact that he didn't do a very good job and someone said out with him and let's get a man in who can do it right.'

'You mean Father.'

'Of course,' said Gretel, who always spoke of Father as if he could never do any wrong and never got angry and always came in to kiss her goodnight before she went to sleep which, if Bruno was to be really fair and not just sad about moving houses, he would have admitted Father did for him too.

'So we're here at Out-With because someone said out with the people before us?'

'Exactly, Bruno,' said Gretel. 'Now get off my bedspread. You're messing it up.'

Bruno jumped off the bed and landed with a thud on the carpet. He didn't like the sound it made. It was very hollow and he immediately decided he'd better not go jumping around this house too often or it might collapse around their ears.

'I don't like it here,' he said for the hundredth time.

'I know you don't,' said Gretel. 'But there's nothing we can do about it, is there?'

'I miss Karl and Daniel and Martin,' said Bruno.

'And I miss Hilda and Isobel and Louise,' said Gretel, and Bruno tried to remember which of those three girls was the monster.

'I don't think the other children look at all friendly,' said Bruno, and Gretel immediately stopped putting one of her more terrifying dolls on a shelf and turned round to stare at him.

'What did you just say?' she asked.

'I said I don't think the other children look at all friendly,' he repeated.

'The other children?' said Gretel, sounding confused. 'What other children? I haven't seen any other children.'

Bruno looked around the room. There was a window here but Gretel's room was on the opposite side of the hall, facing his, and so looked in a totally different direction. Trying not to appear too obvious, he strolled casually towards it. He placed his hands in the pockets of his short trousers and attempted to whistle a song he knew while not looking at his sister at all.

'Bruno?' asked Gretel. 'What on earth are you doing? Have you gone mad?'

He continued to stroll and whistle and he continued not to look until he reached the window, which, by a stroke of luck, was also low enough for him to be able to see out of. He looked outside and saw the car they had arrived in, as well as three or four others belonging to the soldiers who worked for Father, some of whom were standing around smoking cigarettes and laughing about something while looking nervously up at the house. Beyond that was the driveway and further along a forest which seemed ripe for exploration.

'Bruno, will you please explain to me what you meant by that last remark?' asked Gretel.

'There's a forest over there,' said Bruno, ignoring her.

'Bruno!' snapped Gretel, marching towards him so quickly that he jumped back from the window and backed up against a wall.

'What?' he asked, pretending not to know what she was talking about.

'The other children,' said Gretel. 'You said they don't look at all friendly.'

'Well, they don't,' said Bruno, not wishing to judge them before he met them but going by appearances, which Mother had told him time and time again not to do.

'But *what* other children?' asked Gretel. 'Where are they?'

Bruno smiled and walked towards the door, indicating that Gretel should follow him. She gave out a deep sigh as she did so, stopping to put the doll on the bed but then changing her mind and picking it up and holding it close to her chest as she went into her brother's room, where she was nearly knocked over by Maria storming out of it holding something that closely resembled a dead mouse.

'They're out there,' said Bruno, who had walked over to his own window again and was looking out of it. He didn't turn back to check that Gretel was in the room; he was too busy watching the children. For a few moments he forgot that she was even there.

Gretel was still a few feet away and desperately wanted to look for herself, but something about the way he had said it and something about the way he was watching made her feel suddenly nervous. Bruno had never been able to trick her before about anything and she was fairly sure that he wasn't tricking her now, but there was something about the way he stood there that made her feel as if she wasn't sure she wanted to see these children at all. She swallowed nervously and said a silent prayer that they would indeed be returning to Berlin in the foreseeable future and not in a month as Bruno had suggested.

'Well?' he said, turning round now and seeing his sister standing in the doorway, clutching the doll, her golden pigtails perfectly balanced on each shoulder, ripe for the pulling. 'Don't you want to see them?'

'Of course I do,' she replied and walked hesitantly towards him. 'Step out of the way then,' she said, elbowing him aside.

It was a bright, sunny day that first afternoon at Out-With and the sun reappeared from behind a cloud just as Gretel looked through the window, but after a moment her eyes adjusted and the sun disappeared again and she saw exactly what Bruno had been talking about.